UNSPOKEN DESIRES

NATASHA GRACE

Originally published as Fallen in July 2018.

Third Print Edition: July 2021

ISBN: 978-1-955895-01-9

CHAPTER ONE

"Sam! You're here!"

Samantha Collins had just set her briefcase on her desk when she found herself engulfed in a tight embrace by Karen Parker. "Thank goodness you're back. The analysts have been arguing nonstop since you've been gone."

Sam smiled as she pulled away from the bubbly, red-headed accountant. She'd been hesitant about coming back to work and having such a warm greeting eased her worries.

"Knowing them, they're arguing about who has to do the blue-chip stocks." No one wanted to spend their time reviewing boring, stable companies when they could be looking for the next big thing.

But since she'd had no experience in analyzing companies when she'd joined her husband's hedge fund, Harkin Capital Management, three years ago, she'd offered to take those dull companies off their hands. She'd figured there was no better way to learn what separated average businesses from the highly successful ones than to study those that had survived the test of time. To her surprise, she'd enjoyed the work, so she'd continued to do it.

Karen laughed as she raised a hand. "I'm pleading the fifth." After a few moments, she sobered. "How are you holding up?" she asked, a probing look in her brown eyes, and Sam's throat tightened. Though she was grateful and humbled that so many people cared about her, questions like these reminded her of all that she had lost.

"Coming back here is a lot harder than I'd thought," Sam admitted.

It had been two weeks since Jason died, but being at the office made the wound seem fresh. Memories of her husband filled the place, and it was just so easy to imagine him strolling into her office with that heart-melting smile of his, asking if she was available for lunch.

Her chest ached at the knowledge that he'd never do so again, and she inwardly groaned. This was exactly what she'd been avoiding when she'd decided to return to work —the wallowing. It seemed as if all she did now was cry or grieve.

She'd hoped that the work would help keep her mind off of losing Jason, but she'd forgotten that Harkin Capital Management *was* Jason. His personality and vision filled every inch of the office and always would.

"Oh, honey." Karen grabbed her hand and squeezed. "I'm here if you want to talk."

"Thanks. I appreciate it."

Karen gave her an encouraging smile before she gestured towards the door. "I better get going before someone looks for me. It's been so crazy here lately. Let's do lunch when you're up for it."

Once her friend was gone, Sam removed her coat and hung it on the coat rack. A quick glance outside showed that it was still snowing. She'd always loved the winter and everything that came with it—the snow, the hot chocolate… But now all those things were reminders of the icy roads that had taken Jason away from her. She'd never be able to look at snow again without remembering its deadly cost.

Forcing the thought away, she turned towards her desk and picked up the condolence cards that had been left there. As she stuffed them into her briefcase, she spied the annual report she'd abandoned two weeks ago when she'd gotten the call about Jason's accident.

A computer manufacturer she was monitoring had released it that day and, though it was a little late now, she figured she would finish reading that first. Who knew? She might catch something the market had missed.

She had barely finished the second page ten minutes later when the words began to blur. She couldn't concentrate.

All she could think about was Jason and how she'd probably be in his office going over the day's schedule if he were alive. Sighing, she pushed her chair away from the table and walked towards the floor-to-ceiling windows. The Manhattan skyline lay before her, but for once, the view that she'd always admired failed to make an impression. Like the office, the city was filled with memories of her husband.

To the right was the familiar facade of the art deco hotel

where Jason had proposed four years ago. He'd told her that they were meeting a client, but in reality, he'd booked the whole restaurant and had invited all of their closest friends. Then in front of everyone, he'd gotten down on one knee and had asked her to marry him.

She'd been so happy. It had felt as if she'd finally gotten everything she'd ever dreamed of. She'd never expected it could all be taken away from her or how quickly it had happened.

An icy road. Jason driving too fast—

"You're back."

Startled, she turned to find Luke Darren, her husband's friend and business partner, standing in her doorway. He looked exhausted. There were bags under his eyes and his jet-black hair looked as if he'd run his fingers through it quite a few times. As she'd seen so many times over the years when they were working against the clock, his collar was undone, and his tie loosened. But unlike those times, it was well into the morning.

"Have you been here all night?" she blurted without thought.

He rubbed his five o'clock shadow. "Yeah. We just finalized a deal with Leeds."

"Leeds—the grocery chain?" she asked, surprised. Though she hadn't been in one of their stores recently, she'd thought they were doing well. New locations seemed to be popping up all over the city. Had they been overaggressive with their expansion? Was that why they'd approached the company for money?

"Yeah. They were in danger of not making the payroll.

Their entry into Pennsylvania hasn't been going the way they'd hoped."

Guilt that she'd spent the past two weeks at home while Luke had obviously been hard at work dug at her, especially when she realized that she wasn't the only one grieving. Luke hadn't just lost his best friend, he'd lost his business partner as well. And knowing how much of a control freak he was, she was positive he'd taken up most, if not all, of Jason's responsibilities in addition to his already full workload.

"Is there anything I can help with?" she asked and immediately regretted the words. Though they'd settled into a pseudo-friendship over the years, she knew what Luke really thought of her. Hell would freeze over before he admitted he needed her help. He didn't even want her working at the company.

"Yeah," he said and she blinked. Exactly how long had she been gone?

"We're running maintenance on all our holdings and deals. I can have Sheila send you a list of some companies to look over."

Sheila Thompson was Luke's personal assistant and had been with the company for what seemed like forever. Sam wasn't sure where they'd found her, but she'd always thought it a miracle that they'd found someone who wasn't terrified of Luke.

"We're doing all the companies at the same time?"

They usually only did reviews if a new report came out or if some new development arose. Running maintenance on everything was crazy—not to mention a lot of extra work. A company's financials were already reviewed by at least three different people before Harkin bought a single share. To review everything again without any additional information just seemed insane. What exactly was he expecting to find?

A shadow crossed Luke's features. "Yeah. With the Cervco trade and Jason's death, we can't afford to have any weaknesses in our portfolio."

Her stomach dropped at the reminder of the Cervco fiasco. She'd forgotten about that. The software company had been one of Harkin's bigger holdings until it was charged by the Securities and Exchange Commission for falsifying earnings. Overnight, the stock price more than halved. They'd sold all their shares immediately to limit the losses, but the damage had already been done.

Luke's words were a stark reminder that Jason's death had a far-reaching impact. Her decision to take two weeks to privately mourn suddenly seemed selfish when she thought about all the employees Harkin was responsible for —not to mention all the money they'd been entrusted with.

"Sure." She'd help any way she could though she was surprised at Luke's willingness to accept her offer. This was the same guy who'd been so against her working here that he'd lied and told her that Jason had been having an affair. He must really be swamped.

"Thanks. I appreciate it."

"So how's the company been doing otherwise?" She'd heard about two customers pulling their money out. Hopefully, there hadn't been any more.

Luke hesitated before fully stepping into her office and

closing the door behind him. "I think we might lose Peter." Peter Ricci was one of Harkin's top managers. Along with Jason, he headed one of the company's two flagship funds while Luke handled the other. Harkin Capital Management had only consisted of a single fund when they'd first started, but Luke and Jason had soon added more to meet their customers' varied needs. "He's upset that I chose George over him to lead the distressed fund."

"Oh." Though she'd known that Jason's responsibilities would be divided among the remaining managers, it hurt to know that someone else would be replacing him. But that was just the way of things. Life went on even if you didn't want it to. "I'm sorry to hear that," she murmured. Peter leaving the fund would be a blow for sure, but she agreed with Luke's decision.

Though George's returns weren't as big as Peter's, at least he could take criticism and accept when he's been wrong. The chances of another situation like Cervco happening with George in charge was a lot less.

"It's better him than George, right?" she asked, knowing the decision couldn't have been easy. Peter was one of the first employees they'd ever hired.

Luke nodded and took one of the seats in front of her. The silence in her office was deafening as the seconds ticked by and he just stared at her desk. Luke had never been much of a talker, but this was a little much, even for him. She was just about to ask him how Janet, Jason's assistant, was doing when he ran a hand down his face and sighed.

"And around four hundred million has been pulled from the company since Jason's death."

Four hundred million? That was almost a third of what they managed.

"How?" she sputtered.

How could they have lost so much business in such a short amount of time?

"You know that Jason's always been the face of the company."

"But everyone knows about you, too."

Jason had always been showing her articles Luke was mentioned in. Luke didn't entertain interview requests the way Jason had, but people still knew about him and his role in the company.

Didn't they?

"Not as much as they knew about Jason," Luke said, looking pointedly at her.

She shook her head wordlessly. How could Jason's death have caused such an exodus? Though it was true that he was the face of the company and had been a huge part of the fund in the early days, he'd taken a step back in recent years to focus on his charity work, leaving Luke to handle the company's day-to-day operations.

And, sure, many of their clients had been personal friends with Jason, but Harkin's managers were also very good at what they did. Before last year, Harkin Capital Management had beaten the market every year since its inception. Friendship and connections aside, the company made money for their clients. Lots of it. She couldn't imagine them throwing it all away just because Jason had died.

"How could you not have told me?" she finally asked Luke.

If she'd known things had been this bad, she would've come back to work earlier. It might not have been much, but at least she could've tried to help. Remembering that Jason had left his portion of the company to her, she numbly realized that she and Luke were equal partners in Harkin now. She *should've* been there.

"I didn't want you to have to deal with this on top of everything else."

Even Luke was coddling her. She would've laughed if the idea wasn't so ridiculous. He'd never been her biggest fan.

A sudden thought occurred. "Wait—do we have to lay anyone off?" A redemption hit that big would have drastic effects on the company's bottom line.

"As of right now? No. We've always been conservative about our overhead costs. But if we keep losing clients..." He shrugged, and a shudder ran through her. She'd seen so many hedge funds trim their staff over the years. The analysts and the portfolio managers usually ended up okay, but many of the others—like the traders and the administrative staff—didn't. The thought of laying off the people who'd become family to her made her ill. She'd never thought that this could happen to Harkin. The company had always seemed so strong.

"Do you mind sitting in on the Tuesday meeting?" Luke

asked. "George is leading it, but I would feel more comfortable knowing you were there as well."

"You're not going?" In all the time she'd been at Harkin, Luke had never missed the weekly meeting between the company's portfolio managers and analysts. He was just too hands-on a manager to leave it to anyone else. And now, not only was he going to miss one, he wanted her to be his second pair of eyes? Her sense of bemusement increased as she simply nodded in reply.

"Thanks." He smiled as he stood. "I'm really glad you're back, Sam."

A part of her wanted to remind him of a time when he hadn't wanted her here, but she resisted. Rocking the boat would help no one, especially since she planned to continue working at Harkin. The company had meant so much to Jason. She wanted to keep it alive for him.

"I am, too," she murmured and was caught off guard by how much she meant it. She genuinely loved her work and the people she worked with. She *belonged* here. And Luke would just have to deal with that.

CHAPTER TWO

It was time to let bygones be bygones. Or at least, that's what Samantha told herself as she made her way across the trading floor towards Luke's office later that week.

She'd quickly gotten back into the pace of things at Harkin and had made quite a dent in the list of companies Luke had asked her to review. Thankfully, those she'd reviewed so far were in good shape and on course to meet their projected targets.

One of the extra precautions Luke had instituted during the review was to make sure that none of the analysts audited their own work. He'd split up the work anonymously so that they wouldn't know what the others were checking unless they told one another.

It was a smart move, and one she was especially grateful for. She'd always had a suspicion that the other analysts were wary of saying anything critical about her reports because she'd been the boss's wife. Hopefully, the ability to do the analyses anonymously would give them carte blanche to say what they really believed about her work.

Because of their workloads, Sam hadn't seen much of Luke since her first day back, and though they'd always avoided each other in the past, they couldn't continue to do so. Now that they were partners, they had to make sure that they were on the same page, and they couldn't do that if they were never in the same room together. They were going to have learn to get along, and since Luke wasn't in any hurry to change the status quo, it was up to her to reach out to him.

And it was well past time.

Sure, he'd pulled a dick move when he'd lied and told her Jason was having an affair all those years ago. But maybe he'd thought that he'd been protecting Jason somehow. There were a lot of people who believed Jason had married beneath him, and Luke was probably one of them. If that was the case, she couldn't begrudge someone looking out for his friend—no matter how misguided he'd been.

But still, some lingering resentment remained. At the time she'd been appalled at how low he would sink to convince her to leave Jason and therefore, the company. She knew how much Jason had loved her. But for the sake of Jason's friendship with Luke, she'd never told him about the conversation. Instead, she'd distanced herself as much as possible from Luke and had only been polite as was needed.

But everything was different now. Avoidance and politeness no longer cut it.

She sighed as she tightened her grip around the small box in her hand. In it was one of the two watches Jason and Luke had bought after the company had collected their first year's management fees. Even then, they'd known that they were going to be a success. They'd been so confident about it that they'd spent most of the year's earnings on these watches without another thought. It'd been a foolish thing to do, but they'd wanted to make a statement to themselves that the money they'd made that year was nothing compared to what they'd make in the future. And they'd been right. Those extravagant, expensive watches were a dime a dozen to them now.

She figured giving Jason's watch to Luke would show that she was willing to start anew, that they could forge a professional relationship.

The watch was also a thank-you of sorts after all he'd done with the funeral preparations. She would've been a mess if the arrangements had been left to her, and she doubted Jason's parents would've been any better. And he'd done it all without her even asking. The only thing she'd had to do was show up, and for that she'd always be grateful.

It was still early, so Luke's assistant wasn't in yet. Samantha knocked softly on his closed door.

"Come in," his voice boomed.

Well, here goes nothing.

"Hey," she murmured as she walked in. Luke looked up from his computer, his dark eyes widening when he saw her.

"Hey, yourself," he said cautiously.

Was she making a mistake? *Would he misinterpret the gesture?* No. She wouldn't let her worries stop her. He'd been so kind in the weeks immediately following Jason's death and when she'd come back to the office, he'd made sure that she wasn't overwhelmed with too much work.

Besides, he'd worked so hard to build Harkin Capital Management up. If she were being completely honest, she doubted Jason would've reached the level of success he had without Luke. Though Jason was an amazing analyst and portfolio manager, he didn't have the perseverance, the tenacity that Luke did. Luke truly put the company first whereas Jason often got distracted with other priorities.

And sure, it had been Jason who'd gotten them most of their clients, but it was Luke who'd delivered the above-average returns that had kept those clients satisfied throughout the years. And it was Luke who'd picked up the slack when Jason had decided to focus more on his charity work. So, yeah. Luke deserved the watch.

Sam settled in one of the leather chairs in front of his mahogany desk. "I was cleaning up some of Jason's things and thought he would've wanted you to have this." She smiled as she handed him the box.

A curious light entered Luke's eyes as he took it. He froze when he realized what it was.

His throat worked as he opened the box and removed the watch. The overhead LED lights gleamed against the diamonds set in the face as he held the watch reverently.

"I..." He shook his head as he looked at her. "Thank you, Samantha." His voice was thick with emotion, surprising her. He'd always been so stoic.

All the things she'd planned to say about him and Jason being the perfect team suddenly seemed trite. Though they really had complemented each other perfectly—with one's weaknesses being the other's strengths—she could just imagine how many times Luke had heard people say it since Jason's death.

"I'm always here if you want to talk," she said instead.

Sorrow flashed in his eyes. "Thanks. The same goes to you."

She nodded, and a subdued silence filled the room. She glanced at the bookshelf at the side of the room and realized that this was the first time she'd been in his office since he'd told her about Jason having an affair.

She could still recall how his words had upended her world and how hurt and angry she'd been. After months of them not getting along, she'd thought they'd finally become friends. He'd stopped scowling at her and had even smiled at her once or twice. Little had she known that his behavior had just been part of a bigger plan to try to get rid of her. As soon as her defenses had gone down, he'd pounced and fed her lies.

Her back stiffened at the memory and she bolted out of the chair. "I guess I'll let you get back to it then," she said as she gestured towards the work on his desk. Just because she'd decided to forgive him didn't mean that she was ready to forget.

She was almost at the door when Luke stopped her. "Samantha."

Her fist tightened as she slowly turned to face him.

"Thank you," he said as he lifted the watch. "This really means a lot to me."

Sincerity shone in his eyes, and she realized that while Jason may have at times been jealous of Luke, she'd never seen Luke jealous of Jason. It was a disconcerting thought.

"Of course."

* * *

The man was still talking.

Luke Darren resisted the urge to check the clock in the corner of the meeting room later that day. He'd always thought client meetings were a waste of time, but he couldn't afford to offend any more of their customers by refusing to meet them. He'd learned the hard way these past few weeks that some clients wouldn't settle for anything less than talking with the boss. In fact, they felt entitled to it.

Guilt dug at him at the knowledge that he could've stopped some of their investors from pulling out of Harkin if he'd just taken the time to personally talk with them and ease their concerns the way Jason always had. While he understood the importance of client relations, he felt his work spoke for itself. Harkin's excellent returns should've been enough to keep their clients happy without having to entertain them all the time.

He should've known better.

He was already getting rid of all those thousand-dollar-a-plate meals he'd considered legal bribery but Jason had pushed for. The least Luke could've done was meet with the people who'd asked to see him. Instead, he'd sent out a mass email. Not his finest hour.

Hindsight could be a real bitch.

At the time, he hadn't seen the need for all those one-on-one meetings. If the clients weren't talking about topics like yachts or new Broadway musicals, they were trying to fish for information about the company's holdings. It was ridiculous. He hadn't gone through the trouble of making their SEC holdings reports confidential just to blab them to a client.

He was well aware that there were people—including the company's own clients—who tried to mimic Harkin's portfolio on their own to avoid paying management fees. And while it was flattering to have people copy him, it also raised the prices of the stocks they had unnaturally. There had been times earlier in his career when he'd wanted to buy more shares of a company but hadn't been able to because the prices had already been driven up by these copycats.

Hank Randall, who was almost as good as Jason when it came to dealing with clients, was supposed to have been in on tonight's meeting to help guide the flow of the conversation, but his wife's water broke this morning—a few weeks earlier than expected, apparently.

Luke hadn't even known that Barbara was pregnant, and though he was happy for his COO, he wondered why Hank hadn't said anything before today. They spent hours together every day and Hank had never thought to mention that he and his wife were expecting their first child?

"It's a very exclusive school," Thomas Baine, the hotel heir Luke was currently stuck with, said.

Luke wondered what the guy would say if he told him that he'd gone to public school from kindergarten all the way to college. His parents hadn't even been able to afford preschool. Thomas would probably withdraw his money from the fund the first thing in the morning. People like him didn't want to have anything to do with the working class, even though it was their work that had made his family rich.

"Tuition costs forty-nine thousand dollars a year, but it's worth it," Thomas boasted. "They have a student-teacher ratio of four-to-one and it was ranked the best elementary school in the East Coast by *Wealth*. It was really the only school we could've considered for our son."

Luke's eyes twitched. He didn't care what school Thomas had enrolled his kid in or how much it had cost. He just wanted to find a way to wrap up this meeting without insulting another client. He still had a lot to do tonight. He'd recently discovered that Jason had been overleveraging their clients' money in the distressed fund, and Luke was now liquidating some of their riskier assets as fast as he could to mitigate the risk. He hated that he was doing a lot of these trades on intuition and not solid research, but he was pressed for time and didn't have that luxury.

Part of him still had trouble accepting what Jason had done. Though he'd known Jason had lost face with the media when one of their bigger holdings had been caught falsifying their earnings, Luke hadn't thought Jason would renege on their agreement.

When they'd opened the distressed fund, they'd agreed to leverage it by three times at the most. Though it was risky to buy stocks with borrowed money, it was a calculated risk and they'd agreed to manage it extra carefully. Even if one or two companies in the fund tanked, their other holdings would be able to make up for any losses.

But Jason had leveraged the fund by eight. If the market had suddenly turned, his overleveraging would've not only hurt the clients who'd entrusted them with their money, it would've killed Harkin.

"Your son must be very smart," Luke said inanely, forcing himself to focus on the conversation at hand rather than the holdings he needed to sell.

Damn. Could these meetings be any longer? If Hank wasn't able to make it to the meetings Luke had planned tomorrow, George or one of the other managers would have to be pulled in to help ease the conversations along. Luke couldn't risk another disaster like tonight. He could talk business and investment strategies all day, but small talk? Not on his life.

Thomas's chest puffed. "That he is. He's quite bright for his age."

Luke was just about to say, "Like father, like son," when he noticed Sam walking down the trading floor and froze. *She's still here?* It was past seven o'clock. He was wondering if his mind was playing tricks on him when he realized that she was wearing the same dark blue dress she'd worn when she'd visited his office this morning.

Thomas must have seen the direction of his gaze, because he said, "Oh. Is that Jason's wife?"

"Yeah." Knowing that this meeting would soon be dead with just the two of them, Luke stood. "Here, let me introduce you."

He opened the door and poked his head out as Sam approached. Her steps faltered when she saw him, and his stomach dropped. She was still wary of him. He'd hoped that her giving him the watch earlier meant that she'd forgiven him for telling her about Jason's affairs, but perhaps some wounds were just too deep to ever fully heal.

Knowing that this was neither the time nor the place to think about what he could've done differently, he forced the thought out of his mind.

"Hey, Sam. Can you come here a second?"

She hesitated briefly. "Sure."

He caught the scent of vanilla as she walked into the room and tightened his grip around the doorknob. This was *not* the time to be thinking about Sam that way. It never was, he quickly corrected himself. Just because Jason was gone didn't mean that Luke suddenly had a chance with Sam. It didn't matter that his friend hadn't appreciated her the way he should've. Friends didn't steal their friends' wives.

Luke owed everything he had to Jason. He would probably just be an analyst at Brown and Hale right now if Jason hadn't invited him to start a fund. He himself would never have dreamed of owning his own hedge fund. He hadn't had the connections or the money to start one. And as if all that Jason had done for him wasn't enough, he wanted the man's wife as well?

Disgusted with himself, he looked at Thomas as he

made the introductions. "Sam, this is Thomas Baine. Thomas, this is Samantha Collins."

Besides, it wasn't like Sam was interested anyway.

"Hi, Samantha. It's good to finally meet you," Thomas said as he offered his hand. "Jason has told me so much about you."

Sam flashed Luke a quizzical glance before she faced Thomas. "Good things, I hope," she said as she shook his hand, smiling.

Thomas laughed. "Of course, though he didn't mention how beautiful you are."

Twenty minutes later, Luke inwardly laughed as the conversation turned to cooking. Samantha *hated* cooking. As the eldest daughter of two full-time, blue-collar workers, she'd been saddled with cooking duties. Now that she had the luxury of hiring a cook, she, understandably, took advantage.

"So you make your own pasta?" Thomas asked. The question was purely rhetorical because, before Sam could answer, he launched into a monologue about the pasta cutter he'd recently purchased.

Thomas didn't seem to notice that Samantha was faking her interest as Luke had done earlier when they were talking about his son's education. Luke couldn't blame the man. If all of Samantha's attention was directed solely at him, he probably wouldn't even be able to remember his own name.

For what must be the hundredth time, he mentally

patted his back for pulling her into the meeting. Though she might have been hesitant, she'd quickly taken control by engaging Thomas, and for that, Luke was grateful. By putting Thomas at ease, Sam had ensured that he'd walk away confident that all was well at Harkin. Left to his own devices, Luke knew that his inability to make small talk, along with his impatience, would have made Thomas uneasy and convinced that there were problems at Harkin. It wouldn't have taken long for the hotel heir to join the deserters.

It was why Luke needed a wingman—or in the case, a wingwoman—when it came to clients. His strengths lay in numbers and analysis, but where people were concerned, he didn't have a clue. Hell. Even his COO hadn't told him that he and his wife were expecting.

As if she were telling Thomas a secret, Sam leaned forward and pointed at Luke, a ghost of a smile curving her lips. "You might not know it, but Luke, here, does a mean short rib."

Surprised that she remembered that, Luke blinked. He'd made the meal for her and Jason two years ago and hadn't realized it had made any kind of impact on her. Though she'd called the meal "wonderful" at the time, he'd thought she was simply being polite. Was it possible she'd actually enjoyed his cooking? The thought pleased him way more than it should've.

"Really?" Thomas asked as he turned towards Luke. "What's the secret? I've tried making short ribs a few times, but the sauce always ends up being too oily."

"I usually marinate the ribs overnight and then remove

the excess fat before cooking them." He made short ribs the way his mom had taught him and didn't think that there was any secret to them. "The extra marinating really brings out the taste of the wine."

"And what kind of wine do you use?"

"Cabernet."

"Now that's interesting," Thomas said. "I've been using sherry. Have you tried the short ribs at the Jacques Martin? I've been trying to replicate the recipe."

Luke forced a smile as Thomas talked about how his first attempt had overbrowned, then how tough the meat had been the second time. Luke glanced at Sam and saw that she was smiling at him. It was the first real smile she'd given him in years and he couldn't help but return it.

Thomas looked at his watch. "Sorry. I have to get going. My wife will kill me if I miss my son's recital."

"That's all right," Luke said as he bolted out of the chair. "It was nice meeting you."

"You, too," Thomas said as he stood, then turned towards Samantha. "And don't forget to email me that recipe," he said referring to a pot roast recipe Sam had. He patted his shirt pocket. "Did I give you my card?"

"I'll get the info from Janet tomorrow."

He beamed, and Luke resisted the urge to roll his eyes. Sam had probably gotten the recipe from Jason's mom and had never tried it herself.

"Thanks." Thomas turned towards Luke and shook hands. "And thanks again for taking the time to meet with me. I know you're busy."

Luke was about to say, "Anytime," when he remembered how horrible the meeting had gone before Sam had arrived. Though she'd managed this one well, he couldn't count on her willingly participating in any more. Not only did she have enough on her plate as it was, apart from earlier when she'd given him the watch, she usually avoided him like the plague. So instead, he said, "Of course."

After they'd seen the client to the elevator and had started walking towards their offices. Samantha turned towards Luke. "So…that was strange."

"I'm sorry for putting you on the spot, but I was dying in there," he said as he gestured towards the meeting room. Tonight had underscored one of the reasons he'd partnered with Jason. Jason's knack with small talk and pleasantries meant he could deal with the clients while Luke concentrated on what he did best—growing the money.

"I can just imagine." A small smile appeared on her lips as she rolled her eyes, and he tried not to think about how soft those lips looked. "I don't think I've ever seen you meeting with a client. In fact, you're always talking about how meetings are a waste of time and resources to the point of— Oh! I forgot to tell you. Hank and Barbara had a boy. I was on my way to visit them when you stopped me."

The fact that Hank had called Sam but not him niggled at Luke. It bothered him that Hank had never even mentioned that they were expecting. That seemed like big news. News that a guy would share with someone he saw every day. Not wanting Sam to know how out of touch he was with the employees, he said, "That's great. Are you still planning on going?"

"Yeah. The hospital's on the way home anyway."

"I'll go with you." He could just look over the reports George had given him later when he got home.

"I'm sorry. I didn't mean to force you."

"You didn't. I want to go. That is, unless you don't want me to…" With the way she'd smiled at him during the meeting, it was easy to forget that she'd always done her best to avoid him.

"No. Of course you can come. I was just surprised. I didn't think you did things like this."

He didn't, but at the same time, he was enjoying her company and didn't want to leave her just yet. But since he couldn't say that, he shrugged and nodded towards his office. "Let me just get a few things."

CHAPTER THREE

Sam's heart softened as she watched Luke try to decide between a teddy bear with a cute sailor hat and a puppy plush with huge adorable eyes in the hospital gift shop forty minutes later. Even when shopping for baby toys, he was all seriousness.

She was just about to tell him to pick the puppy when he said, "This is ridiculous," then grabbed both of them. She laughed as she followed him to the cashier. She liked that he'd given some thought to what would make the best gift. It was so unlike Jason, who would've just bought one of everything to look good.

Guilt dug at her for the unkind thought, but she knew it was true. Jason had always leaned towards the flashy side of things. That was just the kind of person he was.

Luke grabbed a vase of flowers and set it, along with the animals, on the counter. He pulled out his wallet and turned towards her.

"Do you need anything?"

She shook her head as she lifted the gift bag she was carrying. "I got Charles to pick up some baby wipes and a romance book as soon as I heard." Charles, her driver, had also mentioned how expensive diapers were, so she'd bought a year-long subscription to be delivered to Hank's apartment. But she hadn't even thought to bring a toy for the baby. Knowing that Jason wouldn't have forgotten about the baby, she felt her guilt deepen for thinking badly of him.

"Is that your hospital kit?" Luke asked.

His grin threw her off balance. She couldn't remember the last time he'd smiled at her and today, he'd done it twice!

"It's more of my everyday kit," she admitted. "I always carry wipes in my bag and I have a ton of books on my phone." She never knew when she might have some extra time to do a little reading.

They headed towards the elevator bank outside the gift shop after Luke finished paying.

"So what do you like to read?" he asked as they stepped into an opened elevator.

"I usually read business books or biographies during the week and those really long historical romances over the weekends if I have the time." She loved those lazy days when she could just stay in and escape into a good book. They didn't happen nearly as much as she'd like, but she enjoyed them when they did. "Those page-turners can be real sleep killers."

"I know what you mean. Sometimes I start a book and by the time I know it, it's time to go to work."

"You read?" She didn't intend to sound so shocked. Of course he had hobbies. Everyone did, but she guessed she'd always thought of him as a work machine. He lived and breathed Harkin.

He shrugged. "If I have the time. I love mysteries."

She was still having a hard time picturing him reading for fun. He just seemed too serious a person to enjoy reading fiction. When would he even have the time to? "When was the last time you read a book?"

"Let's see. It was a John Abrams my sister gave to me… Huh. It's been almost two years."

Two years? She couldn't even go a month without reading a book. She must have been looking at him strangely, because he said defensively, "I've been busy."

"I know," she murmured as the elevator doors opened and they stepped into the clinical corridor. She shouldn't judge him because she knew the hours he put at the office. He was there when she came in the morning and was still there when she left at night. Hell, he rarely went out to lunch.

"I can't believe it's been so long since I've read a book," he said as they followed the signs pointing towards the maternity ward. "My parents couldn't afford after-school care, so I used to spend afternoons in the library near my school."

Luke was so successful now that it was easy to forget his harsh upbringing. She'd been thinking that the reason he hadn't approved of her was because of her modest child-hood. In reality, he'd had it worse than her. So if it wasn't her background he didn't approve of, that meant it was *her* he didn't approve of.

Was she just wasting her time trying to patch things up with him? He'd obviously made up his mind about her a long time ago, and his opinion was unlikely to change no matter how hard she tried.

Before she could dwell on the subject further, they arrived at Barbara's room near the end of the hallway. The door was open, but Sam still knocked softly on it before walking in. Hank immediately rose from his seat by the bed when he saw her.

"Sam." There were bags under his eyes, but at the same time, there was a sense of restless energy around him.

"Congratulations," she said as she hugged Hank. Over his shoulder, she saw Barbara flash her a smile as she softly rocked her newborn. Unbidden, jealousy stabbed her. She'd always thought *she'd* have children by now.

In a way, she was grateful she and Jason hadn't had any. She didn't want her son or daughter to grow up without a father. She'd been raised by two loving parents herself and didn't want a child of hers to grow up without the same privilege. But sometimes, the heart didn't agree with the brain. She still found herself wishing that they'd had children. It would've been nice to have a piece of Jason with her.

Knowing that this wasn't the time or place to dwell on what-might-have-beens, she forced the thought away and headed towards Barbara.

* * *

Sam would have been a great mother.

Luke watched her coo over the baby and wondered why she and Jason hadn't had kids. Jason had never shown any interest in having children, but it was easy to see Sam enjoyed them. Had Jason put her off somehow?

Probably.

Luke could easily see Jason cajoling Sam, giving a thousand reasons to delay having kids and Sam accepting them. She'd been such a pushover where her husband had been concerned. Besides, children would have dented Jason's style. He certainly wouldn't have appreciated the time the children would have taken from his affairs.

And wasn't Luke just the greatest friend for thinking the worst of Jason? Sure, he was pissed off at Jason—not just for dying and for leaving Luke with so many messes to clean up, but for all the times Jason had taken Sam for granted. But for all his faults, Jason was a decent guy who'd done well by Luke. He'd do well to remember that.

As he glanced again at Sam's expression while she played with the baby, Luke reminded himself that there was nothing stopping Sam from getting married again and having children in the future. Not only was she beautiful and rich, she was kind and intelligent as well. He was sure there'd be a line of men queued up the moment she declared herself ready to date again—even before.

His stomach dropped at the thought. He didn't know how he would bear it when she started to date again—to see her laughing and smiling in another man's arms. Again.

"I'm sorry I missed the meeting," Hank said in low tones.

It wasn't the first time Hank had apologized this evening, prompting Luke to wonder if he really seemed like the kind of boss who would get mad because an employee needed to be with his wife when she gave birth.

Luke knew he could be a hard boss sometimes, but he hadn't thought that he was *this* bad. Sure, he continuously pushed the employees to do their best, but he never gave them anything they couldn't handle. The fact that Hank was one of the few people at the fund who wasn't afraid of him, who never hesitated to tell him how he really felt, made his sudden deference all the worse. Had Hank been relying on Jason as some kind of buffer? Did Hank think that he could lose his job if he disagreed with Luke on something?

"Don't worry about it," Luke murmured, hoping to ease Hank's mind. He didn't want Hank thinking he was some kind of a monster. "You were exactly where you needed to be."

"So, how did it go?" Hank asked after a moment.

"Horrible," Luke admitted. "Thankfully, Sam walked by around twenty minutes into it and I was able to rope her in."

"Fuck."

"What?" Luke asked when Hank didn't elaborate.

He smiled sheepishly. "I just realized I could've gone to Sam and asked her to meet the clients. It would've saved you the torture."

Immediately after Jason's death, Hank had pushed Luke to meet some of their bigger clients individually, but he'd refused. He'd been busy enough with the transition and had thought that the clients were just flexing their muscles—to see if they could get him to dance to their tune the way Jason always had. He'd naively thought doing a good job, delivering stellar returns would be enough.

It wasn't.

"It wouldn't have been as good as you," Hank continued. "But it would've been something at least."

"No, you were right. The clients wanted me to reassure them. And though I'm sure Sam would've stepped up to the plate, it wouldn't have been fair to her. She'd had enough to deal with as it was."

"Daddy!" A little boy with blond curls came running into the room and launched himself at Hank. As if he'd done it a hundred of times, Hank bent and picked up the boy.

Daddy? The baby wasn't Hank's first?

Footsteps quickly followed, and a man wearing a red sweater appeared at the door.

"I'm sorry, Hank," he said as he held up a pacifier. "The little bugger threw his binky and then took off."

Hank laughed. "That's okay. I know Nathan can be a real handful." He turned towards Luke and made the introductions. "Luke, this is my brother, Jared, and my son, Nathan. Jared, this is Luke Darren, my boss."

"It's good to finally meet you," Jared said as they shook hands. "I've heard so much about you and your magic way with numbers."

Luke wished he could say something similar, but Hank had never mentioned his brother to him. Or his son for that matter. Luke was still struggling with the knowledge that Hank already had a kid. How had he not known that?

"It's good to meet you, too," he said awkwardly as he shook Jared's hand. Man. He really needed to work on his people skills.

"Nathan's getting so big," Samantha exclaimed as she approached and patted the boy's head. The boy smiled before burying his face into his dad's shoulder.

"And heavy, too." Groaning, Hank set Nathan down, and the little boy ran to climb onto the chair next to his mother's bed. Barbara smiled indulgently as she ran her hand through the boy's hair.

Sam laughed as she moved towards Luke. "I guess we should get going."

"Thanks for coming," Hank said.

"Of course," Samantha said. "And congratulations again." She turned to Jared. "To you, too."

Luke threw in his congratulations as well, then headed back towards the elevators beside Sam.

"I didn't even know they already had a kid," he admitted once they were out of earshot and immediately regretted the words. What would Sam think of him? She was so in touch with everyone at Harkin. She always knew whose birthday it was and who had an anniversary coming up. He didn't even know that one of his closest employees was a father.

Sam laughed. "You're not exactly the type of person people are going to confess their children problems to. Besides, Hank isn't like Janet, who somehow manages to work her children into every conversation. He's almost as bad as you when it comes to keeping business and personal lives separate."

Luke knew she was trying to make him feel better, but he still felt guilty. He'd been working with Hank longer than she had and yet, she knew more about the guy than he did. Then there was Hank's apology…

"Am I really that horrible of a boss?"

He knew some of the employees didn't think of him as human, but to believe he'd want them to be at the office when their children were being born?

"Come on." Sam nudged him with her elbow. "It's not like you actually want to listen to everyone's problems about how they didn't get enough sleep because their baby was crying or how their kid's Little League game was cancelled, do you?"

"Of course not. But there's a big difference between knowing about a Little League game and knowing that the person has a kid in the first place." He wasn't a misanthrope. He did care about the employees. He just wasn't doing a good job of showing it.

"You could start asking people more about their days or weekends," Sam suggested. "But let me warn you—people love to talk about themselves."

"That's what I'm afraid of." He had no interest in hearing about people's weekends, but he had to get over his hatred of small talk. Now that Jason was gone, Luke wanted the employees to be able to talk with him if they had a concern, and they wouldn't do that unless he set them at ease.

Tomorrow, he'd make sure he took the time to ask the

employees how they were doing. Hopefully, he wouldn't get any more surprises like secret children who apparently weren't secret at all. He glanced at his watch and saw it was later than he'd thought.

"Do you want to get something to eat?"

"I'm sorry, but I can't. I don't want to keep Charles up too late. We still have to drive back." Sam lived in Greenwich, which was still almost an hour away.

He was about to tell her that he could drive her but stopped. One week. She'd been back at the office only one week and he was already pushing work aside to spend time with her. He never did that. Hell, he didn't even accept dinner invitations from his family when he was busy at work, and his family meant everything to him.

With Harkin on such shaky ground, he needed to put his all into the company—not think of ways he could spend more time with Sam.

The realization triggered a wave of regret and he realized that he'd only been fooling himself when he'd told himself he was over Sam. He still wanted her. He'd never stopped.

The guilt hit him hard. Jason may not have been the best of husbands, but he'd been a good friend. And how did Luke repay Jason? By envying him his wife and telling Sam about Jason's affair.

Only, it had backfired. Sam had refused to believe Luke and had stood by her man. It had taken years before she'd bothered to be anything more than chillingly polite to Luke. And still, he wanted her.

Because he knew he'd do something stupid if he

continued to spend time with her, he vowed to keep his distance as best he could. So he said goodnight at the hospital entrance and watched as Charles drove her away in her black SUV.

But as he went home, feeling empty, he wondered how he would ever manage to stay away from her.

CHAPTER FOUR

Luke parked in front of his parents' home and sighed as he took in its tattered roof and old window shades. He'd been wanting to buy them a house for years, and when they'd finally given in, they'd chosen this?

Even after all the renovations he'd had done, Luke still felt as if it would be easier to just tear the whole thing down and build a new house.

Though he was happy that his parents were finally living in a safer neighborhood, he wished they'd let him do more. What was the use of having all this money when he couldn't help the people that he loved? Hell, the only reason they'd even agreed to move was to be neighbors with old friends who'd recently moved here as well.

Shaking his head, he glanced at the passenger seat and felt his heart soften when he saw that his sister was still asleep. She'd probably had a lot of late nights studying for her finals next week, and though he was so proud of her— not only was she the first in the family to go to graduate school, she'd also be the first doctor in the family—he felt bad at the knowledge that things would only get worse from here. She'd start her residency next year and, from what he'd heard, thirty-hour shifts were the norm, not the exception. It wasn't the kind of life he wanted for his baby sister, but since it was what she wanted, he'd support her in any way that he could.

He hated to wake her up from her much-needed sleep, but everyone was already waiting for them inside. He shook her shoulder lightly. "Wake up, Anna."

When she didn't wake up, he shook her a little bit harder and she turned towards him.

"Are we there yet?" she asked, her eyes barely open.

"Yeah."

She covered her yawn as she stretched. "I'm sorry, Luke. I must be the worst passenger."

"It's fine." He actually enjoyed the quiet time to think about the company's problems but doubted his sister would appreciate him saying so. He got out of the car and got the French vanilla ice cream he'd had his cook make out of the cooler in the trunk. It would go well with whatever pie his mom had chosen to bake.

"Is it bad that I already want pie?" Anna asked as she joined him.

"I've been looking forward to it all week," he admitted with a grin. After his younger brother had moved out for college, their mom had instituted a monthly dinner ritual to make sure no one drifted away, and without fail, she always made pie.

The door opened as they made their way up the steps, revealing their brother holding a beer bottle.

"It took you long enough," Brian said and Luke inwardly rolled his eyes. His brother was perpetually hungry. It was probably why he'd decided to move near Mom and Dad after college—he could drop by their house for lunch and then again at night for dinner.

After their parents had moved to the new house, Brian had complained about having to worry about lunch every day, but Luke knew that he still went to Mom and Dad's for dinner almost every night.

"Brian!" Anna rushed to hug him.

Brian returned the hug. "How's school going?"

"It's the worst. Thank goodness I'll be done next year."

"A Darren through and through," Brian said, laughing as he messed with Anna's hair.

Both Luke and his brother had hated school, but they'd been forced to go to college, because their parents had refused to settle for anything less for their children. They'd wanted more for their kids than the factory and waitressing jobs they'd had all their lives.

"As if there was any doubt." Anna elbowed Brian before she went to join Dad on the couch.

The sound of sneakers squeaking against the floor blazed from the TV. Luke looked into the living room and frowned when he saw that Dad was watching a basketball game.

"When did Dad start watching basketball?" he asked his brother.

"Ever since Tracy Howard got drafted."

Luke tried to place the name and came up empty. "Should I know who that is?"

Brian smiled as he clamped an arm over Luke's shoulder. "He was a few years behind Anna at Jefferson High. Ended up getting drafted last year. He's only been in, like, four games, but you know how it is."

Luke nodded. The community supported their own even if the player was a benchwarmer.

"It's almost done!" his dad yelled from the couch and Brian laughed as he walked towards him.

"You've been saying that for the past thirty minutes."

A smile tugged at Luke's lips as he crossed the living room to the kitchen. Some things never changed. He walked into the kitchen and found his mom pouring spaghetti sauce over the noodles.

"Hey, Mom," he said as he approached her, mindful not to startle her. He'd accidentally made her drop a meatloaf when he'd been younger and while everyone had been forgiving, he'd never forgotten how hungry he'd gone to bed that night.

"I brought ice cream," he said as he gave her a sideways hug.

She grabbed his arm. "Thank you, dear. It will go perfectly with my blueberry pie."

Mmm. Blueberry.

He liked the sound of that. He let go of her and went to put the ice cream in the freezer. He had just closed the freezer door when his mom hugged him again. His heart softened as he wrapped his arms around her. He'd missed her as well.

"I just wanted to get a proper hug," she murmured as she stepped back and gestured towards the large bowl of pasta on the counter. "Now set that on the table and call everyone for dinner."

They had barely finished grace fifteen minutes later when his mom asked, "When are you going to get married and give your father and me grandchildren?"

Not again.

Luke looked at his brother for help and saw Brian grinning at him. Knowing that he wouldn't get any help there, he looked at his dad, who'd grown a sudden interest in his salad. Damn. He knew that his dad wanted grandchildren, too. He was just more subtle about it.

Way more subtle.

"Mom. I'm only thirty-four," Luke finally said. Just because his parents' friends were grandparents didn't mean that they needed to become grandparents as well.

"Hmph! You know, I was twenty-one when I married your father," she said as she pointed a fork at him.

"I know."

He and his siblings had heard all about their parents' love affair hundreds of times over the years. His mom was working at a diner when his father had come in after a tough day at the factory. One look at Mom, and Dad had forgotten all about his day. It had taken him a week of going back to the diner every day for a soda pop—because that was all he'd been able to afford—before he'd finally gotten the nerve to ask her out. It had only taken six months of dating for his dad to propose although Dad always said that he'd known he was going to marry her the moment he first set eyes on her.

Mom shook her head as she turned towards Dad. "I just don't know what it is with kids these days. They're always putting careers before family."

"I just haven't met the right woman," Luke said, though he knew he didn't have time for a relationship, either. He didn't even have the time to read. And with all the withdrawals they were experiencing, the company had to be his top priority right now. Because if Harkin went down, it was taking him along with it.

Harkin Capital Management would just be another name in the list of hedge funds that had come and gone, and no one would ever trust him to handle their money again.

"Right woman?" his mom parroted. "You know too many women—*that's* the problem."

No, not too many women—just one. An image of beautiful brown eyes flashed in his head before he pushed it away. He was not going there. It was bad enough that he'd wanted Sam when she'd been married. He wasn't going to make the situation worse by pursuing her now that Jason was gone.

"There haven't been that many women," he protested while Brian laughed. He raised his eyebrows at his brother. "You do know that you're next, don't you?"

"There was Rhonda—" his mom ignored them as she started counting on her fingers, "—Veronica, and then there was Angela..."

Knowing that he'd never brought home any of those women, Luke turned to see his sister suddenly avoiding his gaze.

When had everyone turned against him?

Had Anna done an internet search on him then told Mom? No. His sister didn't even have time to sleep. It was more likely that Mom had asked her to do a search on him. She could be so nosy sometimes.

He was about to say that those women had been a one-time thing before he realized how that sounded and stopped himself. His mom didn't need to know about his sex life—or lack thereof.

"They just didn't work out," he murmured.

At the time, he'd thought that seeing other women would help him get over Samantha, but if anything, it'd just made things worse. He'd found himself comparing everyone to Sam and had found them all lacking. What's worse was the realization that most of these women didn't see him for himself. Instead, they saw the billionaire and the life of luxury he could provide them.

He couldn't help but compare them to Sam, who could've had the life of luxury these women wanted after marrying Jason. Instead, she had joined the company and worked just as hard as the other employees—sometimes even harder, as if she were trying to compensate for being the boss's wife.

"I almost forgot—Sam!"

Luke froze. Was his mom seriously asking him if he felt something for Sam? Had he been too obvious? He'd always been conscious not to mention her too often, but he guessed he hadn't been careful enough.

"How is she doing?" she asked.

Of course. Mom was just checking up on Sam—not asking if he was interested in the woman.

"Okay. She's already back at work." He took a big gulp of water and tried to get his head on straight.

"That's good to hear. We were so worried about her."

"I still can't believe that he's gone," Anna said softly. "Jason always seemed bigger than life, you know?"

"I know." The way Jason had swept into his life twelve years ago still seemed unbelievable sometimes. This trust fund kid had had huge dreams, and he'd been willing to share them with him. Luke was well aware that Jason would've had plenty of other choices if he'd looked—analysts and portfolio managers who'd had the experience and the knowhow—and yet, Jason had chosen him. Someone he'd met when they'd both been doing an internship at Brown and Hale.

Almost overnight, Luke's life had changed. After growing up with never having enough, he suddenly had more than he would ever need and for that, he was eternally grateful. He would never again have to worry about whether or not he could afford a warm meal or if he could pay next month's rent.

The reminder of just how lucky he was to have had the opportunity for a better life—not only for himself, but for his family as well—made him even more determined not to squander it. He'd build Harkin back up and recoup the business that they'd lost if it was the last thing he did.

CHAPTER FIVE

"Oh, my goodness," Nina Hall said as she put down the empanada she'd just taken a bite of. "This is amazing. You *have* to try it."

"Thanks, but I'm really stuffed," Sam admitted as she eyed all the plates on their table. She couldn't remember ever being this full—it felt as if she were drowning in food. Nina, who'd arrived at the restaurant first, had practically ordered the whole tapas menu for dinner. On top of everything that was out already, there were still a couple more orders in the kitchen that had been held back because there hadn't been any space on the table.

Nina's eyes narrowed. "You just want to save room for dessert, don't you?"

Sam laughed at the unexpectedness of the statement. Her friend and former roommate knew her well. Even when she was full, Sam was always up for dessert.

"Okay. I admit that I *was* looking forward to the chocolate cake, but I think I'm going to need a few minutes—or an hour—for everything to settle down first."

"Hmph! I bet you wouldn't even hesitate to take a bite if the waiter put a cake in front of you right now."

"As if there were any room. What were you thinking ordering so much?" Though Nina often missed lunch—as a corporate lawyer, she often got so busy that she forgot to eat then binged later—this was a little much. Even for her.

"I guess I overreacted. With Andrew spending the night and all the work in the office, I haven't eaten since lunch yesterday and that was just a salad."

Sam froze. "You mean Andrew—the same Andrew you met at a Christmas party a few weeks ago? The guy gave your number to?"

"Yeah."

"I can't believe you didn't tell me you were seeing someone! How could you not have told me? I called you like the minute Jason asked me out."

The fact that Nina was just telling her about her new relationship stung. Sam didn't have a lot of close friends— sure, there were plenty of acquaintances and people with whom she was friendly, but no one like Nina.

They'd hit it off immediately when they'd met in a calculus class in college and had become fast friends. Over the years, their friendship had become a rock in Sam's life, the thing she could count on regardless of how often they saw each other. That Nina had withheld mentioning her new boyfriend hurt. Were they not as close as Sam had believed?

"I meant to tell you," Nina said, her tone sounding

contrite. "But you were always busy and then with Jason…"

The guilt hit hard. It was true—she'd often been too busy to see Nina. Trying to fit in a lunch or dinner between the two of them had become an exercise in futility these past few years. There were always meetings and galas she had to accompany Jason to, and when she was free, Nina was stuck at work or out with a client. They'd eventually resorted to making do with phone calls and text messages—only seeing each other if there was an occasion.

If she was being honest, she hadn't actually wanted to come tonight when Nina had texted her earlier, asking if she was available for dinner. But at the same time, she hadn't wanted to go home to an empty house again. Though she was fine for the most part, Jason's death always hit the hardest when she arrived home from the office alone. So she was surprised when she'd found herself enjoying the evening and catching up with her old friend. She'd have to make a better effort to see Nina from now on.

Noting the sudden hesitation in Nina's expression and guessing that it had to do with Jason's death, Sam sighed. People were still walking on eggshells around her, and it was getting tiresome. Wanting to go back to the easy conversation they'd had minutes earlier, Sam forced a smile as she grabbed her friend's hand.

"Fine. I forgive you. Now, tell me everything about Andrew."

* * *

"Tonight was so fun," Nina said over the phone almost two hours later. As promised, Sam had called Nina when she'd arrived home to reassure her friend of her safety. It was another fall-out of Jason's accident—friends and family were more worried about her than they'd ever been before. "We have to do it again soon."

"I agree," Sam said as she climbed the marble staircase. After the long day, she was exhausted and wanted nothing more than to lie down and rest. "Just not at the same place. I'm pretty sure that the restaurant put us both on some kind of do-not-serve list after tonight." Or at least, had implemented a dish limit of some sort.

"Hmph. Their ribs were a little dry anyways."

They hadn't been, and Nina knew it.

"I still can't believe we were both free tonight," Sam murmured as she walked into her bedroom and turned on the lights.

"I know, right? I don't even remember the last time we went out. I think I was still on the Matterson case." A beep sounded. "I'm sorry, Sam. I got to go. Miranda's calling. Call me!" Nina made a smooch sound then hung up.

Sam threw her phone onto the bed and reached for the straps of her heels. She breathed a sigh of relief once the shoes were off. *Finally.* She would've worn flats if she'd known that Nina would invite her to dinner, but she'd thought she was going straight home after work.

She settled in against the pillows on her bed and frowned at how easily she'd settled into life without Jason. *Shouldn't moving on be harder?*

She'd been with Jason for five years. She should have

felt as if a huge chunk of her was missing. Instead, she was going out with Nina as if nothing had happened. She winced when she thought about how much fun she'd had tonight and felt even worse at the knowledge that she wouldn't have been able to go out with Nina if Jason had been alive. She'd probably still be at a gala or a dinner meeting right now.

Suddenly remembering the bag of personal effects the police had given her after the accident, she went to the closet to get it. Worried that she'd dissolve into a mass of tears, she hadn't dared look through it, but perhaps it would do her some good to remember her husband.

She settled back on her bed and opened the bag, spying the leather wallet she'd given Jason for Christmas last year. Her chest tightened as she traced over the initials she'd had engraved onto it. She'd been so worried about whether or not he would like it. Buying presents was hard enough on its own, but to buy them for someone who could afford anything he wanted? It was downright impossible.

But all her worries had disappeared the moment he'd opened the box and she'd seen the warmth in his eyes. Remembering the way he'd told her he loved it and the way that he'd kissed her afterwards, she blinked back tears.

How could he have left her all alone?

Sure, he'd always driven a little faster than the speed limit, but he should have known to take care of the icy roads. Now all that she had left were memories. Realizing that she was gripping the wallet, she let it go and spotted Jason's cell phone—the phone that had been like another limb to him.

If he wasn't working, he was helping out with one of the many charities he was involved with. Wanting to remember that side of Jason—instead of the careless, selfish side that had him speeding on dangerous roads—she picked it up and turned it on. The phone buzzed with message notifications.

She swiped right and clicked the first message she saw —a message from Carla Williams, the director of one of the charities Jason had worked with and immediately dropped the phone as if it were on fire. She'd been expecting charity talk—maybe plans for the upcoming gala or updates on their school program. Instead, there were pictures of Carla wearing lingerie!

There must be some mistake.

Sam's mind scrambled for an explanation. Carla had probably texted Jason instead of her husband by accident. Or maybe her husband had left the phone in Jason's car. Sam picked the phone up again and scrolled through the messages, looking for something that indicated that it was Carla's husband's.

But there was none.

Her stomach dropped when she saw a text where Carla had called him "Jason baby." As Sam started to read the conversation, it became clear that not only had Jason encouraged the woman, he'd even bought the lingerie she was wearing!

The phone slipped from Sam's hand once again. *How?* How could Jason have done this to her? Hadn't he loved her?

Her chest tightened, and she suddenly found it hard to

breathe. *Was this why he'd kept on delaying having children?* It wasn't that he'd wanted to wait until he had the time to be the kind of father his dad was. Because he'd apparently had enough time to have an affair.

He just hadn't wanted to be tied down to *her*.

She sobbed at the realization. She'd been such a fool. A complete and utter fool.

An hour later, when all her tears were gone, only anger remained. Five years. Five years she'd given that man. Five years of galas, power breakfasts, tedious business dinners, paparazzi—all because she'd wanted to be a good girlfriend and then, wife. And he'd repaid her loyalty and commitment like this?

She'd even given up her dream job at Anderson for him. Because no one wanted an accountant whose husband was a hedge fund manager. That decision had hurt—she'd loved that job and enjoyed the people she worked with—but she'd been okay with it, because she'd loved Jason and would've done anything to be with him. But it turned out she'd been the only one who'd felt that way.

Shaking her head, she looked unseeingly at the bedroom. Suddenly, the house that had once been her dream home felt like a mockery of everything that she'd ever wanted. She couldn't stay here another minute. Without bothering to pack a bag, she put her shoes on, grabbed her purse and headed towards the garage.

CHAPTER SIX

Luke had just finished putting the last of his dishes into the dishwasher when he heard a knock on his door. Knowing that he hadn't let anyone up, he groaned. The last time he'd gotten an unexpected visitor like this, it had been a neighbor who'd been trying to get Luke to buy his house in the Hamptons. Apparently, the man's bonus had been smaller than he'd been expecting.

Perhaps Luke should've been more sympathetic to the man's plight, but it was hard to sympathize with someone who, in addition to his apartment downstairs, had three vacation houses and four cars that were each worth more than Luke's childhood home. Some people just didn't know how good they had it.

Luke went to check the peephole and blinked when he saw Samantha. *Why hadn't she used the private elevator?* He quickly opened the door and felt his chest tighten at the sight. Though she was as beautiful as always, there was a sense of gloom around her. Her shoulders were slumped and the eyes he'd always admired were full of misery. He'd never seen her like this. Even at the funeral, she'd seemed so strong. Now, she looked defeated.

"How did you know?" she asked him in a small voice.

He frowned. "Know what?"

She swallowed visibly and lifted her chin. "About the cheating."

Luke froze. *She wanted to talk about that now?* He'd told her that years ago and she'd promptly called him a liar, which he'd deserved. Though he hadn't lied, his intentions hadn't been honorable, either. He'd wanted her for himself and, in a twisted moment, he'd thought that he'd finally get a chance with her if he just told her about Jason's affairs.

His gut tightened at the realization that she must've found something while going through Jason's things. He couldn't even begin to imagine what she was going through. To lose a husband then find out that he'd been cheating on her? She must be devastated.

"Because he told me," he finally said, knowing that there was no way out of it. He wished he could spare her the pain. No matter what he'd done, he'd never wanted to hurt her.

His heart broke as Sam took in his words and nodded stiffly. She didn't deserve this. She was such an amazing person, and to see her used like this was unconscionable. Luke wished he could take her in his arms and comfort her, but since it was a bad idea to go anywhere near her, he resisted.

He wished he was stronger—to be the kind of friend that she needed, but he wasn't. She twisted him inside in a way no other woman ever had and, frankly, he didn't trust himself around her. He always wanted more when it came to her.

He watched silently as she drifted to his couch and sat down, staring mutely at the floor. She looked so lost and small.

"Did he…" She swallowed then raised her head to look at him. "Did he love her?"

Luke groaned. She thought Jason had only been seeing one woman?

And maybe he had been by then. Luke certainly wouldn't know. Not wanting his friend to find out how he felt about Sam, Luke had always done his best not to comment or ask about the affairs.

But it had killed him to watch Sam kiss Jason goodbye, knowing that she thought her husband was going to a meeting, when in reality, Jason had been going to meet other women. To then hear Jason bragging when he came back to the office had been too much. After one particularly bad day, Luke hadn't been able to control himself from telling his friend exactly how he felt about the way he'd been treating Sam.

Jason had chalked off Luke's outburst to his having a sister and Luke hadn't bothered correcting him. He'd known that he'd crossed the line. After that, Jason had never mentioned the conversation or his conquests to him again.

"No, I don't believe he did," Luke murmured as he joined Sam on the couch. In some ways, Jason hadn't cared about anyone but himself.

Sam shook her head. "But three years..." Her eyes widened as she turned towards him. "There was more than one woman, wasn't there?"

Not knowing what else he could do, he nodded.

"How many were there?"

He ran a hand through his hair and shrugged. "I don't know." At one point, it had seemed like there'd been a new woman every week, but he was sure Jason must have cooled down in recent years since no one had come forward to make a quick buck after his death. Unless, they'd all been married...

Tears filled Sam's eyes before she looked away. "I feel so stupid," she said, her voice breaking. "I mean, I should've known. He was barely at the office."

"I think that Jason was very good at pulling veils over all of us." He would have never thought that Jason would go behind his back and overleverage their clients' money, but he had. The fact that Luke's trust in Jason was the reason he hadn't caught it sooner just made the situation all the worse.

"It's so crazy. I mean, why did he even allow me to work in the office if he was going to cheat on me?"

Luke hesitated, but since she'd come to him for answers, he told her the truth. "I think he wanted to keep an eye on you. He was, er...beginning to think that you were cheating on him."

It sounded ridiculous—even to Luke. All anyone had to do was look at Sam's adoring eyes whenever Jason was in the room to know how she felt about her husband. She would have never cheated on him. Besides, she just wasn't that kind of a person.

Her eyes widened. "Me?"

"You know how paranoia works." Eventually, the cheater begins to think he's being cheated on as well. "How did you find out?" he couldn't help but ask. She hadn't believed him then, so why did she believe it now?

Sam looked down as she played with the hem of her green dress and he tried not to think about the fact that he was so close to her that he could see the the weave of her stockings, the translucent material making him itch to touch her—to run his hands over the legs he'd spent countless hours thinking about. Shame poured over him. She was hurting and here he was thinking about how smooth her legs would feel? Disgusted with himself, he clenched his hand and forced himself to look away.

The silence in the room was deafening. He was beginning to think that she wasn't going to answer his question when she spoke.

"I wanted to feel closer to him, so I went through the bag of things the police retrieved from the car. His phone was filled with texts from Carla Williams." She winced. "I think I even hugged her at the funeral."

Fuck. It was bad enough to be cheated on, but to be cheated on with someone she was probably friends with? It was unconscionable. How could Jason and this woman have done that to Sam?

Luke wished he knew the words to make her feel better, but it had always been Jason that had been good with words—not him.

"I'm sorry," he finally said, and had never felt so inept

in his life. He wanted to tell her that she was a strong and amazing woman, and that Jason had never deserved her, but he wasn't sure how she would take it.

"No. I'm sorry I didn't believe you," she said, her voice suddenly earnest as her head rose and her gaze met his. "It was just so much easier to believe that you were trying to get rid of me." He winced at the memory of how badly he'd treated her when she'd first started working at the company. He hadn't given her any reason to trust him. "It feels as if I've just wasted these past five years of my life," she continued.

"I wouldn't say that. You turned out to be a pretty good analyst."

She groaned as she covered her face with her hand and he belatedly remembered that she hadn't wanted to work at Harkin any more than he'd wanted her to initially. He'd questioned her ability to contribute to the team—she was an accountant by training, not an analyst—and hadn't wanted Jason to get distracted by her.

Instead, he'd been the one distracted.

He never knew how she'd gotten so under his skin. He'd gone from resenting her presence at the office to admiring her work ethic. Eventually, he'd told himself that he should find a woman like her and the next thing he knew, he'd wanted Sam for himself.

"It's not a nightmare, is it?" she asked, her voice painfully soft as she turned towards him.

He shook his head and wished there was something he could do to take away her pain, but this was just something that could only be healed with time.

She sighed as she stood up. "I'm sorry for bothering you this late, but you were the only one I could talk to."

He frowned as a sudden realization occurred. "You didn't drive here by yourself, did you?" he asked as he stood as well.

"I did, but it's okay. There was no traffic."

There was no traffic? Was she insane? She was in no condition to drive even if there were no cars. Terrifying thoughts of what could've happened to her filled his brain and he was grateful nothing bad had occurred. He'd just lost Jason. He wasn't sure he could handle losing Sam as well. Even though he knew that she wasn't for him, he needed her to be all right.

He didn't want to argue with her—especially not now— but at the same time, he wasn't going to let her drive tonight. "Let me drive you home."

"No. That's fine. I'm going to stay in a hotel."

"Then I'll drive you there."

"You don't have to, but thank you for the offer. I really appreciate it."

"I'm not letting you drive tonight, Sam." He'd never forgive himself if something happened to her.

She laughed softly. "I never realized how much you looked out for people." She sighed as she looked down for a moment before meeting his gaze again. "I'm sorry for calling you a liar all those years ago. You didn't deserve that."

Guilt pricked his conscience at the knowledge that he hadn't told her about Jason's affairs out of the goodness of his heart. He'd wanted her for himself and didn't deserve her forgiveness for his act of selfishness. But since there was no way of correcting her without revealing his feelings for her, he remained silent.

She glanced at his door. "Is it okay if I stay here tonight? I—"

"Of course," he interrupted, grateful that she'd gotten the idea of driving out of her head.

For the sake of his sanity and willpower, it probably wasn't a good idea to have her so near, especially now that Jason's secrets were no longer between them. But Luke knew that she'd be safe from him tonight. No matter what he wanted, he would give her the space she needed. And if the temptation to go to her became too much, he'd go to the office.

Relief shone in her eyes. "Thanks. I really don't feel like facing a lobby of people right now."

"I understand. I'll show you the spare room."

Had he even loved her? Had he ever?

Sam groaned as she rolled onto her side. It had been an hour since she'd climbed into bed, and Jason still filled her thoughts. She had to stop. He obviously hadn't cared for her—at least not enough to be faithful. So, why was she even wasting another second thinking about him?

Because I love him.

That's why.

She had to be eight kinds of stupid for loving that cheating bastard, but love didn't just disappear because she'd discovered he'd been cheating. She wasn't sure if it ever would.

She sighed as she turned onto her back and stared at the darkened ceiling. Had their relationship been doomed from the start? She couldn't help but remember all of the worries that had begun to bug her once she'd accepted his proposal. Things that she'd never thought about when they'd dated began to plague her. She was suddenly worried about whether or not she was good enough for him, if she could keep him happy, and about other women hitting on him. On top of being handsome and kind, he'd been rich and well-known as well. There were bound to be women who'd be after him regardless if he was taken or not.

After driving herself crazy for weeks with those fears, she'd made the conscious decision to trust him. Any other way would've just been setting herself up for a life of misery, and she hadn't wanted to let her insecurities get the best of her.

And then this happened.

Hell, even Luke had told her that Jason had been cheating on her and instead of believing him, she'd called him a liar. How could she have been so blind to her husband's true nature? How could she not have seen what was right in front of her?

Jason had never even bought lingerie for her.

It was such a silly thing to fret about, but she couldn't help herself. Over the years, she'd often bought lingerie to surprise him in bed, to keep the spark alive between them. And he'd never, not once, bought anything of the kind for her—his *wife*. Yet, he'd bought lingerie for Carla, and possibly others as well!

Another wave of pain hit Sam. What was wrong with her that Jason hadn't thought of her when he went to lingerie shops? Had he stopped being attracted to her? Was that why he'd sought out other women? Was she not sexy enough? Charming enough?

What did Carla have that she didn't?

Her fists tightened as tears threatened to come out. She hated that he could make her feel less of a woman. She'd done nothing wrong except have bad taste in men. If he'd wanted out of the marriage, he should've asked for a divorce—not go behind her back. Instead, he'd chosen to cheat on her repeatedly. While she'd been at home, being the dutiful wife, he'd been out with anything that had legs!

Was their lack of prenup why he hadn't wanted to get a divorce?

With his team of lawyers, Jason must've had at least one person recommend a prenup, but he'd never asked her to sign one. She'd thought a lack of one showed his dedication to her, but in hindsight, she guessed it was probably because he hadn't wanted to do anything that could be seen as a lack of confidence. He'd hated being doubted.

But he must've regretted not getting a prenup afterwards or why else would he continue to stay married to her when he clearly enjoyed the single life? Or had the fact that he'd been cheating excited him?

She shook her head. After years of not understanding why some women tried to get as much as they could during divorce settlements, she suddenly understood. They were hurt and angry and wanted a way to lash back at the men who'd put them in this situation.

The funny thing was that she wouldn't even try to take him to the cleaners if he were alive right now. She'd wasted enough time on him as it was although she would've dearly enjoyed throwing a drink in his face. She could just imagine him worrying about staining one of his bespoke suits or Italian loafers. Or better yet, to watch his face as she scratched those cars he loved so much.

But he'd even robbed her the satisfaction of doing that.

She hated that she wouldn't get even a tiny bit of revenge. It wasn't fair that he'd cheated on her for who knows how many years and got away with it scot-free. Where was the justice in that?

Her thoughts drifted to Luke. Though he'd never said it, Jason had always been jealous of Luke. Not only did the media cover Luke without him chasing them the way Jason had, but Luke's returns at the company had always trumped Jason's. It was probably one of the reasons Jason had focused more on charity work. It was the one arena where he wouldn't have to compete with Luke. Luke would kill himself before he was caught rubbing elbows with the elite.

How would Jason feel if she slept with the man he'd been so envious of?

She could just imagine his face turning red at the thought of Luke one-upping him once again, and she smiled. Sure, Jason would never know about it, but it would feel so good to get this little bit of revenge—to get back at him somehow.

No. She could not—would not—have a one-night stand with Luke. Before tonight, she'd been convinced he was a liar who hated her. Even if she could get over her embarrassment about believing the worst of him for so long, there was no way Luke would accept her advances. Just imagining how hard he'd laugh kept her exactly where she was.

Still… Luke was a very good-looking man. She'd always thought so but had let her anger with him prevent her from admitting it, even to herself. Without that anger holding her back, she could appreciate his sexiness. He'd looked so deliciously rumpled and approachable on the couch tonight. She'd wanted to take comfort in his arms and let it buffer her against the truth that hammered at her. She imagined running her hands over that wide chest of his…

Goodness. Could she really have sex with Luke? She imagined how his naked body would feel against hers and shivered at the thought.

Yeah, she definitely could.

Butterflies fluttered in her stomach as the idea began to take root. She'd never had a one-night stand before, but if anyone deserved it, it was her. And why shouldn't she? She was single, and so was he.

But it was Luke—Jason's partner and the man she'd been angry at and cool towards for years. Would he have sex with her as some kind of revenge for the way she'd treated him? No, somehow, she knew instinctively that she could trust him, that she would be safe with him. She'd never seen him act out of revenge or wounded pride.

And the fact that he never got serious about anyone

worked in her favor. He wouldn't make this into something it wasn't. It would just be sex.

There was nothing holding her back.

Giddy at the thought, she headed towards the living room, wearing only the shirt Luke had loaned her, and was surprised to see the lights still on. She didn't stop to think. She'd only chicken out if she did, and she did not want to spend any more of the night thinking. Her heart skipped a beat when she saw Luke standing behind the dining table as he read a report. She could do this.

She started towards him. As if sensing her, he looked up. His eyes softened when he saw her. "Having trouble sleeping?"

"I—" Remembering that she was supposed to be seducing him, she stopped. "You're still working," she said instead as she approached him. She shouldn't be surprised, but she was. He already spent most of his waking hours at the office, and when he finally went home, he still worked? It was no wonder the company was as successful as it was. The man was a machine.

His lips twisted as he looked at the papers in front of him. "Yeah. I'm just trying to figure something out."

Guilt that she was bothering him while he was obviously hard at work bit at her before she forced it away. It was three o'clock in the morning. He should be in bed—not working. Jason surely wouldn't have been working right now if he'd been alive, and she suddenly realized how unfair Jason's habits had been to Luke.

"Well, you don't have to finish this all tonight, do you?" she asked in what she hoped was a seductive voice as she placed a hand on his chest. His very hard chest. She felt heady at the thought. Without giving him a chance to answer, she wrapped an arm around him and kissed him before she lost the nerve. His lips were soft, and the fresh, clean smell of him was intoxicating. Wanting more, she brushed her tongue against his lips.

Mortification assailed her when she realized that he wasn't kissing her back.

And why would he? She'd just shown up on his doorstep, dumped all her problems on him, and then asked to spend the night here. And how did she repay his kindness? By jumping him.

Cursing herself, she was about to step away and apologize when he groaned and shoved his hand into her hair, deepening the kiss. Her mind blanked of everything except the feel of his lips on hers and the way his tongue danced with hers. *Yes.* This was what she was looking for.

Loving the way her body molded into his, she pushed herself even closer to him, running her hands greedily over his back, admiring the hard muscles underneath. His hands ventured lower, pressing her body into his. His hardness brushed against her and heat pooled between her legs.

Wanting nothing between the two of them, she began unbuttoning his shirt. Electricity buzzed through her as he made a line of kisses down her throat, his stubble scratching deliciously against her skin. He found the sweet spot below her ear and then, as if he were intent on driving her insane, he sucked it, then bit it, laving his tongue all over it. She moaned. *So good.* He felt so good.

She had to touch him. As soon as she had uncovered

enough of his chest, she stopped unbuttoning to run her hands all over it, taking delight in its hard contours. She peppered kisses over his chest and he pulled her in for another mind-bending kiss.

His hands dipped below the hem of her shirt, sending waves of pleasure coursing through her as he splayed his palms across her stomach. More… She wanted more of his touch. With a sudden deft move, he took off her shirt. Her first instinct was to cover herself, but she resisted. She wasn't going to allow doubt to cloud any part of this night. This night was for her alone and hopefully, for Luke as well.

Luke's eyes darkened as he looked at her, making her breath catch. No one had ever looked at her like that—as if she were a dessert he wanted to gobble up—and she found the idea intoxicating.

"Beautiful," he rasped. "You're so fucking beautiful."

Oh my.

Before she could respond, he lifted her to sit on the table and stepped between her legs. He wrapped one arm around her, pulling her chest towards him.

"Oh." Pleasure wracked through her body as he laved her nipple with his greedy tongue. She ran her hand through his hair, encouraging him, keeping him close, and he gently bit her in response. "Oh. Luke."

* * *

Sam's voice grounded Luke into reality. He released her breast and looked up. Male satisfaction coursed through him at the sight of her swollen lips and the lust in her eyes. He'd done that to her. He wanted to do even more things to her, but something stopped him.

"Is this your way of getting back at Jason?"

He was a fool for asking, but he needed to know that she felt at least a fraction of what he felt—that this wasn't about revenge. Sparks of electricity coursed through him as she ran her hands down his chest. Hell. He might already be past the point of no return. He felt as if he would die if he didn't get another taste of those sweet lips soon.

But he wouldn't play a part in any twisted revenge scheme. However complicated his feelings about Jason were right now, Luke couldn't be with Sam for the wrong reasons. He deserved more. *She* deserved more. And her silence was telling. Although he should have expected revenge to be her motivation, it still felt as if he'd been kicked in the gut.

All those times he'd imagined being with her, he'd always imagined that she wanted him, too. It was a foolish thing to want—especially when all he'd ever wanted was right here in front of him—but she had to want him for himself. Calling himself ten times stupid, he released her and was about to take a step back when she stopped him.

"Please," she said as she wrapped her arms around him, her bare breasts pushing against his chest. "I feel like less of a woman, and I hate that he's taken that away from me. I want this. I *need* this."

His chest tightened. She'd never needed him before, and he found himself wanting to be the one who erased all the pain Jason had caused her. Luke gingerly cupped her face and kissed her. And as her taste exploded in his mouth, he realized that he would never get enough of her.

She broke the kiss and moved lower, dropping tantalizing kisses and licks over his chest. Dreaming. He had to be dreaming. That was the only explanation he had for Sam touching him, kissing him. Not wanting to wake up from this delicious dream, he picked her up and headed towards his bedroom. As if she couldn't get enough of him either, she continued kissing him as she ran her hands over his chest and back. It was too much and yet, not enough.

Sensor lights turned on as he walked in and for that, he was grateful. He didn't want to miss a single thing. Setting her on the bed, he licked her nipple before scraping it with his teeth. Her eyes fluttered as he took the nipple into his mouth. Moaning, she arched off the bed, her nails digging into his back. His cock hardened even more. *She was so sensitive.*

He made his way down her flat stomach with kisses, loving the sound of her labored breathing. He eased her panties off and opened her long legs. His head lightened when he found her wet—wet for him.

He had to taste her. She gasped when he licked her. She was so sweet. He greedily drank his fill, loving the way her soft moans filled the air. And when she was close, he wrapped his lips around her and groaned when she came.

Knowing that he might never get the chance again, he continued, licking and sucking, letting himself get drunk on the taste of her. The sound of his name on her lips drove him wilder and he quickened his pace. Her legs began to tremble. She soon came again, crying out his name.

He needed her *now*.

He straightened and removed the rest of his clothes, then got a condom. His hands shook as he put it on. Some part of him still couldn't believe that this was actually happening—that this wasn't a dream. After years of wanting her, Sam was finally in his bed. What had he ever done to deserve this? In disbelief, he looked up to make sure she was still there and caught her watching him. It wasn't just someone with her hair or her eyes—it was actually *her*.

His head lightened when he saw the desire in her eyes. She liked what she saw. The thought that Sam would want him in any way was a heady one. He couldn't get back to her quickly enough. Soon, his hands were on her and he was kissing her as if he were a man starved. She let out a soft gasp as he entered her, and it was the sexiest thing he'd ever heard. *So good. So fucking good.*

Delicious sensations coursed through him as they found their rhythm. Her eyes closed as she wrapped her legs around him and moved against him. Pure satisfaction coursed through him as he watched her lose herself to the sensation. Damn. There was nothing sexier than seeing a woman pleasured, and the fact that it was Sam? It was the sexiest thing he'd ever seen and ever would.

Too soon, he found himself nearing the edge. Not wanting to come without her, he was about to reach for her clit when she screamed. The feel of her tightening around him was too much. He came, pouring himself into her.

Groaning, he laid his forehead on hers, making sure not to crush her as he caught his breath. Her breasts rose and fell as she caught her breath, and he was captivated by the sight. He would never get enough of this woman.

He reversed their positions, letting her sprawl over him then began running his hand over her arm. He knew that he should take care of the condom, but he didn't want to move just yet. She just felt so good in his arms. And perhaps, a part of him worried that she would disappear the moment he let go of her. So, he remained where he was, enjoying everything for as long as he could.

CHAPTER SEVEN

Feeling unbelievably amazing, Sam stretched as she woke up. She froze when she realized that there was a body underneath her. A very hard one.

Luke.

Her breath caught as she opened her eyes and saw his handsome face. He had one arm wrapped around her and the other above his head as he slept. Taking the opportunity to look at him without him knowing, she took in his soft dark hair, that strong nose, and those lips that had kissed her so thoroughly last night. Her gaze ventured lower to his five o'clock shadow, and a shiver coursed through her as she remembered how his stubble had felt against her skin as he'd kissed her.

Mortification assailed her when she suddenly remembered how clingy she'd been. He'd tried to get away from her and she'd grasped onto him as if he'd been her last hope. Ashamed, she made a move to get out of bed when his arms tightened around her and before she knew it, he was pulling her up for a kiss. Her toes curled as pleasure coursed through her before she remembered herself. She ended the kiss and was surprised by the fierceness in his eyes.

"Don't say it," he warned. "Don't tell me that last night was a mistake."

"I wasn't," she said. "Last night was…" She struggled to find the right words. It had been amazing and surprisingly intimate. Maybe it was because of everything that they'd talked about, but she'd never felt so close to anyone. "Last night was just what I needed," she finally said, though that fell short of what the night meant to her.

She couldn't help but worry about where sex put the two of them now. She'd been hoping that they would be friends, but after last night, she doubted she'd get that wish. They'd probably just end up avoiding each other again, which made her feel just awful. Not only had she used him last night, she'd probably thrown away her last chance to be friends with him.

And for reasons she didn't understand, having him as a friend seemed desperately important right now.

He seemed to relax and nodded at her. "I want to see where this will go."

"You want to see where this will go?" she parroted dumbly before realization sunk in and horror coursed through her. Did he think he needed to make a relationship work between them to prevent any awkwardness at the office? Because that was the only explanation she could think of for why he was trying to make this something that it wasn't. The company meant everything to Luke and she could easily see him doing damage control on anything that might hurt it.

"Luke, we don't need to do this. I think we're both mature enough to not make this something that it clearly isn't." She didn't need him to pretend to feel things he didn't. She'd had enough of that with Jason, thank you very much. "Last night was just sex," she told him then tried to lighten the mood. "Amazingly great sex—"

He crushed his lips over hers before she could say more. The kiss was hot and demanding, and she knew she was hooked. She would never get enough of his kisses. His hardness dug into her.

"Does that feel like just sex to you?" he asked, his eyes fierce.

Her breath caught, and he cursed as he pulled away. At a loss, she watched as he sat at the edge of the bed and ran a hand through his hair. Her throat dried as she watched the muscles in his back stretch from the movement. Why did he have to be so sexy? Though she knew she should get out of there as soon as possible, all she wanted to do was wrap her arms around him and tease him back into bed. She couldn't think of anything better than spending the day in Luke's bed.

"Don't tell me last night meant nothing to you," he finally said as he turned to face her.

Her throat tightened at the realization that he'd truly felt something last night. He wouldn't be so insistent if he hadn't. Something warm slowly unfolded within her, soothing the wounds of Jason's carelessness that were still so fresh and raw.

But no matter how tempting it was to throw caution to the wind and embrace what Luke was offering, she knew that she was nowhere near her right mind to start a relationship. And he deserved better than that.

She shook her head softly at her own inadequacy. "I'm sorry, Luke. I'm just not ready for another relationship." With the way she felt right now, she wasn't sure if she ever would be. Though she knew that all men weren't like Jason, she doubted she'd be willing to take the risk again. This pain, this sense of not being enough, hurt too much.

Luke's jaw tightened as he looked away.

"I am, too," he said after a moment before he stood and left.

She felt the strong urge to follow him, to throw caution to the wind and give in to what they both desperately wanted, before she reminded herself that none of his relationships ever lasted more than a single night. Hell. After all these years that she'd known him, she doubted that she'd ever seen him with the same woman twice. He'd tire of her sooner or later and she knew instinctively that that would break her.

Sighing at the futility of this situation, she went to the bathroom to freshen up before she got dressed.

* * *

Stupid. Stupid. Stupid.

Luke slammed the coffee maker shut. What had he been thinking? That after one night, Sam would suddenly realize that he was the man for her? That she'd suddenly return his feelings after hating him for so long? Insane. He had to be certifiably insane. That was the only explanation for the way he'd suggested she give them a chance.

Fuming, he tightened his hand around the handle of the carafe as he poured water into the machine. It didn't matter that she'd kissed him as if she'd been dying for the taste of him last night or that she'd felt so right in his arms. Not only had she just lost her husband, but she'd also just found out that that lying bastard had been cheating on her. Of course she wasn't ready for a relationship.

Oh, but that didn't stop Luke from wanting one with her with his every being or wishing that he could change her mind. Guilt dug at him at the knowledge that he was using Jason's affairs as an excuse to not feel guilty about last night. Just because Jason had cheated on Sam didn't mean that she was up for grabs. What made it worse was the knowledge that he wouldn't even have had last night if it hadn't been for his selfishness when he'd told Sam about Jason's affair. But he figured he was more than paying for it.

To have had her for one night and to never be able to again… He groaned. He'd always thought watching Sam make eyes at Jason had been hell, but this was a million times worse. To know how sweet her lips tasted but to never be able to kiss her again? It was downright unbearable.

"Hey." He looked up and felt his heart skip a beat when he saw Sam walk into the kitchen wearing one of his button-down shirts. She had it loosely fastened with the hem ending just a little past her hips, giving him an eyeful of those long legs of hers.

"I hope you don't mind. I borrowed another one of your shirts."

Since she hadn't brought any clothes, he'd given her a shirt before she'd gone to bed. He'd wanted her to be comfortable and perhaps, he'd also liked the idea that something of his was touching her skin. He'd never thought he'd have the pleasure of taking it off her as well. Hell, she could borrow any of his shirts as long as he got to see her in them.

"Yeah. Of course," he murmured as he tried not to think about how easy it would be to rip that shirt off. She only had a few buttons fastened. All he had to do was pull and it would be gone. But she didn't want him, and he had to learn to live with that. Again.

His fist tightened as he tilted his head towards the coffee maker and asked as casually as he could, "Coffee?"

If he had anyone to blame, it was himself. He should've had better control over himself last night. But how could he? After all these years, the woman of his dreams had finally been in his arms and he'd wanted. So damn much.

"Yeah. Thank you."

He poured two cups of coffee and added milk into one. She frowned as she accepted the mug with the milk.

"You know how I take my coffee?"

He knew everything about her, but since that would sound weird, he shrugged. "How long have we been working together?"

"Jason didn't even know," she said quietly as she looked into her cup.

He wanted to say that it was a sign to give him a shot, to

show that he wasn't like Jason, but he didn't want to smother her. So instead, he said jokingly, "Perhaps you should make it a requirement for the next guy."

"Probably." She laughed as she brought the cup up to her nose and sighed. "It smells divine. Thank you."

He smiled. "It tastes even better."

She grinned and blew into her cup, cooling the coffee. The sight of her pursed lips had his cock stirring, and he forced himself to look away. Would he ever stop wanting her? Was it even possible? He'd wanted her for so long that it just felt like second nature to him. It was probably why he'd never let himself get serious about another woman. There'd only been room in his heart for one and it had been Sam.

"Do you want to stay for breakfast? Maria—"

"Actually, I should get changed and get going," Sam interrupted. "But thanks for the offer."

"Of course," he said, trying to not let the hurt dig into him. It looked like they were back where they started. With her avoiding him.

That was great. Just fucking great.

* * *

Sam stared at the TV, barely taking in the movie she'd rented in the hotel room. After she'd left Luke's place, she'd gone shopping for clothes before checking in. She'd thought watching the action flick would keep her mind off of things, but she just couldn't concentrate enough to enjoy it.

All she could think about was Jason and how foolish

she'd been. All this time, he'd been cheating on her and she hadn't even realized anything was wrong! How could she have been so blind, so trusting?

She'd never made a fuss when he wanted to hang with the boys and had even supported him when he'd wanted to become more active in the community. Oh, how he must have laughed at her! It was almost as if she'd given him a free pass to cheat with all her attempts to be a good wife.

When she started dating again, she vowed that she would never let another man make a fool of her. She wouldn't let herself become the pushover she'd been with Jason.

When she dated!

Knowing that the only reason she was thinking about dating again was Luke, she groaned. Though she'd refused his offer to see "where things would go," she hadn't been able to get it off her mind. She'd been sorely tempted to say yes, but she'd known that there was no way she'd ever be able to keep his interest. How could she? She hadn't even been able to keep her own husband's! Besides, her head was in such a mess right now. She couldn't drag Luke down along with her.

Some part of her still couldn't believe that she'd used him the way she had. She never did stuff like that, and for it to be Luke just made things all the worse. He'd been so kind—not only in telling her about Jason all those years ago, but in being there for her yesterday.

He'd even offered to drive her home, and instead of appreciating all that he'd done for her, she'd used him. Shame washed over her at the memory. Sure, the sex had been the best she'd ever had, but it had also ruined what would've been the beginning of a new friendship. How was she ever going to face him again? What must he think of her?

She should've just stayed home last night or better yet, gone straight to the hotel. What exactly had she been hoping for? That Luke would deny her accusations? That he'd have an excuse for all the pictures and texts she'd seen on Jason's phone?

Now, instead of putting all this behind her, she'd just made things worse with Luke!

Sam reached for the remote and turned off the television. She had to start thinking about the future and where her life went from here. She'd start with getting a new apartment. Because there was no way in hell she'd stay in the house she'd shared with Jason. The house that had once represented all her dreams of having a family and growing old with him was now a testament to how gullible she'd been. She couldn't live there. Instead, she'd get an apartment in the city—far, far, far away from that house.

She scrolled down her contacts on her phone until she reached a Realtor whom she was friends with. She paused before dialing. Calling a Realtor to look for an apartment sounded like something Jason would've done. He never took care of the nitty-gritty details when he could assign them to someone else. All he had to do was snap his fingers and people went running.

Not wanting to have anything to do with Jason, she thought about how she'd looked for an apartment pre-Jason and remembered that she'd searched online first and figured she'd start there. Even if she didn't see anything she liked, at least she'd be more prepared about what she wanted. Decided, she opened the browser on her phone and did a search for available apartments in Manhattan.

And that decision, however small and insignificant it was, felt empowering. As though, after a very long time of being dormant and letting someone else make the decisions for her, she was finally taking charge of her own life.

CHAPTER EIGHT

"Good morning, Mrs. C."

The security guard's welcome gave Sam pause Monday morning. She'd been on the fence about coming to work all weekend. On one hand, she hated the thought of continuing to work at the fund Jason had created, hated having any more of her life dictated by that lying cheat. But on the other, she loved her job and felt as if her leaving the fund would be letting him win somehow. She needed to do what was best for her and not let her anger at Jason lead to rash decisions—like how she'd seduced Luke Friday night. So instead, she was trying to think through things before taking action.

But Ruben's cordial greeting cemented the fact that she'd always be Jason's wife to everyone here.

It didn't matter that she worked her butt off to be the best analyst she could be. She'd always be the woman who'd gotten the job because her husband was the boss. Hell, she even owed her office with its perfect view of

Bryant Park that she loved so much to Jason. Even after all the promotions she'd gotten at Anderson, she'd still had to share a cubicle with another accountant.

And she didn't even want to think about the long security lane she'd just bypassed and the private elevator she was about to enter. It seemed as if her life was a list of privileges she'd gotten because she'd married Jason.

Sighing, she stopped and smiled at the security guard. "Good morning, Ruben."

"Did you see the game last night?"

"No, but I heard it went into overtime."

Ruben shook his head. "You missed a good one, Mrs. C. Hill did twenty-five points."

"Considering his salary, he should be making thirty." She wasn't really interested in professional sports, but she'd picked up a few things from Jason. Ever since she'd corrected a player's name for him in front of Ruben, the security guard had begun talking sports with her as well.

Ruben smiled. "It's only his second year. Wait another year and he'll be doing forty!"

"All right. I'll hold you to that," she said as she stepped into the private elevator, her heart heavy with the knowledge that Jason tainted everything here. Even her conversation with the security guard linked back to Jason. How could she continue working here, knowing full well that Jason had practically hand-fed her everything? She'd never be her own person if she stayed.

Her anger returned as the elevator rose. And to think, right after he'd died, she'd actually wanted to continue working at the fund to keep his spirit alive! If she'd never found those texts, had never found out about his cheating, she would've continued playing the role of a loyal widow.

With sudden clarity, she realized that she couldn't continue working at Harkin. Her love of her job and her friendship with her co-workers would always be overshadowed by Jason and how he'd controlled her existence at the company. Yes, she'd allowed it, but she wouldn't do so any longer. She had a choice now, and she wanted, *needed*, to be her own person. Completely separate from him. And that meant leaving Harkin.

A weight lifted off her chest even as the decision saddened her. She'd talk to Luke as soon as she could about her leaving the company.

* * *

"Luke! You're just the person I wanted to see."

Luke's heart skipped a beat as he turned towards Sam. He hadn't seen her since she'd left his apartment Saturday morning and he'd missed her—her dark, silky hair that he'd loved shoving his hands into, those beautiful brown eyes that fluttered in pleasure when they became one… Please say that she was going to give him a chance. He'd never ask for anything again.

"Hey, Sam."

"Can we talk somewhere private?"

Despite the crazy beating of his heart, he somehow remained outwardly calm. Hopefully.

"Sure." He glanced around the busy trading floor. The meeting room was empty, but the clear glass walls wouldn't give them any privacy and he was dying to kiss her—to have her in his arms once again.

"Let's go to my office," he said. It wasn't as close, but at least they'd get some privacy. He resisted the urge to wrap his arm around her as they made their way there. It wasn't something he'd usually do and he doubted she wanted to parade their relationship in front of the employees.

Once his office door was closed, Sam turned towards him. "I want to sell Jason's half of the company."

His head snapped back as though she'd slapped him. *She wants to sell?*

This talk wasn't about her giving him a shot. This was about her severing the only connection he had with her. His stomach dropped at the thought.

She was getting rid of any reminders of her old life—including him.

Her sudden decision to sell was proof that he'd only been a convenience Friday night, a means for her to feel better after discovering Jason's lies. And though he'd known that their one night together hadn't meant as much to her as it had to him, the realization of just how little it mattered to her hurt.

It had been the best night of his life.

Almost as an afterthought, he realized how badly her leaving the company would look for him professionally. The press was already making it seem as if he didn't know what he was doing—one journalist had even insinuated that Jason was the brains behind Harkin and had advised his readers to pull their money out of the company. They'd interpret Sam's departure as a sign that she didn't have confidence in him running Harkin, either.

He shook his head. "Sam—"

"Fifty million," she said softly but firmly.

Fifty million? That was less than what they made in management fees in a year. She must really want to leave to not have even asked for a year's earnings.

"Half to me now," she continued. "And the other half to a couple of charities staggered over the next few years."

Even with everything that was going on, she was still thinking of other people. He would've laughed if he wasn't so miserable.

Needing time to think, he went to sit down at his table. It was times like this he wished he kept liquor in his office.

"I'm sorry, Sam, but I just can't risk anything right now," he said once he got his bearings. "Maybe in a quarter or two." He had to make sure business stabilized before he committed to any large financial decisions.

"I'm not staying, Luke," she said with a fierceness that surprised him. As if realizing how harsh her voice had become, she stopped and softened her voice. "I can't continue working here where I'll be reminded of him everywhere I go."

"I'm sorry, Sam," he said, ignoring her bit about Jason. He hated that memories of Jason would be always be here for her, hated the thought of Jason taking any more than what he already had from this amazing woman. "But I'm not paying fifty million for half of a company that might not even exist a year from now." He knew he was making things hard for her, but the company had to be his top priority.

"Is it really that bad?" she asked as she took the seat across from him.

"You know how much of a hit we took from the Cervco fiasco last year. Jason's death just made it all the worse." He sighed before adding, "And there's another reason I can't buy you out right now. Shortly after Jason's death, I found out that he'd been overleveraging the distressed fund. We've liquidated a big portion of the holdings, but we still have a long way to go. I was planning on deploying our cash reserves if something wrong happened."

Well, what was left of their cash reserves. With all the redemptions the company had suffered, their cash holding, which had always been stronger than most in their industry, was strained.

"I'm sorry I didn't tell you sooner, but I didn't want you to think less of him." Emotion flashed in her eyes and he could guess she was probably thinking about how she could leave in the midst of all this. Wanting to ease her worries, he said, "Give me six months. If everything's good by then, I'll buy you out." The thought of her leaving made him uneasy, but he understood that this was something that she needed to do to move on. He just prayed that she would realize how much she loved her work and decide to stay.

She hesitated before finally nodding.

"And do you mind staying two weeks for the transition?" he asked, knowing that her departure would be messy. Though she mostly worked as an analyst in the corporate debt fund, she also had a finger in almost every department in the company.

"I… Of course." Gratitude and relief shone in her eyes, and he knew that he was only fooling himself in hoping that she would change her mind. She'd leave as soon as she could without a single glance back.

"How do you want to play this out? Do you want to go with you needing time off as your reason for leaving?"

"I guess." She shrugged and frowned. "Maybe we can say that I've decided to step away from the company to focus on charity work?"

"Sure. With all the donations you're planning to do, I doubt anyone would question you. I just need to talk with Hank before we announce anything. Can we talk later today about how we should divvy up your responsibilities?" With Harkin the way it was right now, he didn't want to hire any new people.

"Sure."

A heavy weight settled on Luke's shoulders, wearing him down. He just couldn't catch a break. First, with the Cervco fiasco, and then with Jason's death. And as if that weren't enough, Sam was leaving now, too. And though her departure wouldn't be as bad for business as the first two, personally, it was devastating. Seeing her had always been one of the bright spots of his day. He couldn't imagine not having her there. He didn't want to.

Worried that he would make a fool of himself and try to change her mind, he cleared his throat as he stood up. "I have a client meeting in a few minutes. I'll drop by your office later so we can work out all the details."

"Sure. All right."

He smiled grimly as he led her out the door. He needed a drink. Perhaps he'd bring the client to the bar down the street. Though it wasn't as if he could get plastered during working hours, a drink could help numb the pain of Sam's departure.

* * *

"Now, are you sure you don't want to talk to the interns?" Ross asked Sam the next day after she'd told him she couldn't teach the financial analysis workshop anymore. They were announcing her departure later today, but she'd wanted to give the analyst a heads-up since the internship program was starting next week.

She'd taught the introductory class the previous two years and had been planning on doing so again this year. But since she was leaving, Ross would either have to teach the class himself or find someone else to help him.

"I'm sure." She would still be here when the program started, but she figured it was best not to meet the interns at all. She didn't want them to become familiar with her and then feel abandoned when she left. Besides, she was sure that one or two of the other analysts would enjoy playing mentor to the interns if given the chance. Though the analysts at the company weren't exactly the nurturing type, she doubted they'd mind having an intern or two look up to them.

"How about dropping by for a chat?" Ross asked.

A grin tugged at Sam's lips. The man was such a

worrier. He didn't even let himself get excited when the fund managers bought a stock based on his recommendation. He usually ended up worrying about the stock's performance and whether or not the manager had bought the stock "too soon."

"I'm sure you'll do fine," she told him. "If you're really uncomfortable, get someone to help you. I'm sure Joanne or Chris would be happy to help."

He grabbed a notebook and a pen. "Why don't we use EBITDA again?" he asked as he waved his hand. "I mean, I know why, but I like the way you put it."

She knew that ignoring EBITDA went against what a lot of business schools taught, but it was just a lot of white noise to her.

"Because there's no reason to use it," she said. "It just makes earnings appear larger than they really are. Interest, taxes—" She stopped when she saw him scribbling like a madman. "Would you rather I send you an email?"

The relief in his eyes was almost palpable. "Yes, please."

She laughed. "Okay. I'll put something together and send it to you by the end of the day." She grabbed his hand in reassurance. "Relax. You'll be fine."

"Easy for you to say," he said accusingly. "I still can't believe you're abandoning me."

She resisted the urge to roll her eyes. He was acting as if she were leaving him with a bunch of toddlers.

"There'll only be five of them." He groaned, and she laughed again. "Call me if you need anything."

She felt the familiar hum in her veins as she stepped onto the trading floor. She was going to miss this, she thought as she walked back to her office. Instead of feeling empowered, as if she was getting her life back, she felt as if she was deserting the co-workers who'd become family to her. Though hedge fund managers and analysts weren't particularly known for their warmth, she'd gotten close to quite a few of them, possibly because they hadn't seen her as competition.

She'd been the boss's wife, who'd been expected to leave once the children came, and she'd assumed the same. Setting her own hours was a big reason why she'd accepted Jason's offer to join the company in the first place. She'd figured she'd get to control her work hours and still be there for her children in whatever way they needed.

Since both her parents had worked full-time jobs, neither of them had ever gone to one of her piano recitals or any of her other school activities. She'd always envied her classmates when their parents had come out to support them and knew that when she became a mom, she wanted to do everything—to be there for games, to drive them to practice, and to even help with homework.

But the children had never come.

Jason had somehow always found a way to delay. First, he'd said that he wanted to have a honeymoon period without any children, which she'd thought was romantic. Then when she'd pressed again last year, he'd said that he was too busy at work to start a family—that when he had children he wanted them to be his top priority.

Little had she known that he had had the time, he'd just had other priorities. Her fists clenched as she thought about all the years she'd wasted on him. Regardless of how she felt about her job and the people there, leaving to start anew was definitely the right decision.

As she neared her office, she got an idea and headed towards reception. She smiled when she opened the door and saw the young blonde behind the front desk. "Hey, Theresa. Will you order lunch for the whole office?" Hopefully, food could temper the news that she was leaving.

"Sure. Where from?"

"Your choice."

Theresa's eyes widened. "Are you serious?"

"Yes. Just don't make me regret it."

"I won't. Wow. Thanks, Samantha!"

"You're welcome," she said, glad to have made someone happy today. Guilt pricked at her at the knowledge that the happiness probably would be short-lived. She could already imagine Theresa's stricken face when Luke made the announcement later today.

With luck, the young receptionist wouldn't be that hurt. Who knew? Maybe Sam was overestimating how close she and the employees really were. "And please charge it to my personal account."

Yes, lunch would be a good way to soften the news and ease her guilty conscience.

CHAPTER NINE

Luke had just stepped onto the trading floor the next morning when he saw Hank coming towards him. His COO's expression was grim. Instinctively, Luke knew what the problem was.

"We lost another client," he said, preemptively, as Hank stopped in front of him. He knew that the recent reprieve had been too good to be true. They hadn't lost any customers since last week and he'd been hoping that they'd seen the last of the withdrawals.

"We actually lost two today."

Fuck. How much more business were they going to lose? It was hard enough to work with what little capital they had left, not to mention demoralizing for the managers. He could already see some of the guys close to breaking.

"Which ones?" he asked.

"One of the pension funds in New Jersey and NorCal."

"Please don't tell me it's the teachers' pension." The

New Jersey Teachers' pension fund was worth around eighty million.

"No. It's Dayner."

Luke's chest eased a little. Dayner's pension was probably around twenty million at the most, but NorCal was a lot bigger—three times as much. They couldn't afford to lose any more customers or there would be cutbacks. When he'd run the numbers last night, he'd seen that the company would barely break even if they had similar returns as they had last year. With the loss of these two clients, Harkin would firmly be in negative territory unless they cut down on their expenses, which was mostly payroll. And he did not want to fire anyone over something that was his fault. It was one thing to fire an employee because they weren't performing, but to do so because of something that was out of their control? It was unthinkable.

"Open the funds to new clients," he instructed his COO. Not wanting to take riskier investments just because they had more money to manage, they'd closed Harkin to new investors two years ago. Hoping that things would turn around, Luke had held back on opening the funds after Jason had died. He hadn't wanted word of people pulling out to spread and have the customers who'd stayed with them begin to worry as well. But it was a risk they had to take if he didn't want the company to go through massive layoffs.

A shiver ran down his back at the thought of no one wanting to invest with them before he quickly cursed himself. He was overreacting. Of course, there would still be people who wanted to invest with Harkin. Who wouldn't after all those years of solid returns? He just needed a few months for people to see that they'd overreacted and then everything would be okay. It had to.

"Do it as quietly as you can," he told Hank.

"Of course."

And this was just the tip of the iceberg. There would soon be more to worry about when NorCal signed with another fund. Since it would be a huge feat to get one of Harkin Capital Management's customers, the new fund would undoubtedly shout it from the rooftops the way Jason had gone a little crazy with the press releases when they'd gotten NorCal from Tyco Enterprises.

Hank hesitated before he spoke. "Have you thought about locking the funds?"

Luke blinked in surprise. Though he had thought about it, he couldn't believe that Hank had really just asked that. Preventing their customers from withdrawing their money —even if it was only temporary—would make his job, not to mention everyone else's, that much harder by having to deal with angry clients on top of everything.

Hank must really be worried about Harkin to have recommended *that*.

"I did, but decided against it," Luke answered. "Even if we hit record returns for our clients, they'll leave the second they're allowed to." Though it wasn't as if their clients actually needed the money, no one wanted to be denied access to their funds.

Hoping to ease Hank's worries, Luke forced a smile as he started for his office. "Thanks for keeping me posted. I expect we'll be getting more foreign investments than pensions this time around." He would rather build up the retirement accounts of hard-working Americans than the already rich abroad, but beggars couldn't be choosers.

Hank scoffed as he followed him. "Only you would think about that at a time like this."

His response reminded Luke of how different their backgrounds were. While Hank hadn't come from old money like Jason had, he hadn't come from a poor one, either. Hank didn't know what it was like to work for more than forty years and have only a company pension to rely on for his retirement. He didn't understand how the higher returns they earned for pension funds made a world of difference for those pensioners. They could retire a year or two early, help pay for their children's education, or even pay their medical bills.

"There's nothing wrong with wanting to help people." Luke thought about how his dad wouldn't have had to work so hard for so long if the hedge fund managers in charge of his pension hadn't screwed up so badly. If it weren't for hedge funds always trying to outdo each other with big returns, his father would've been able to retire at the age of sixty-four instead of working to the bone at the factory.

"And this is how they repay us," Hank said as he gestured towards the trading floor.

Like Jason, Hank had always been more in favor of catering to rich clients. There were a lot less paperwork and requirements and they got to rub shoulders with the rich and the powerful. But what was the use of making the rich even richer? At the end of the day, they were just filling already full coffers.

"Come on," Luke said. "It's not like the pension funds are the only ones who've pulled out." Some of their wealthy clients had left as well. It was just because of the larger size of some of these pension funds that made it seem like they were the biggest offenders.

Perhaps he shouldn't have fought Jason so hard about closing Harkin to new clients two years ago. They might not be in such a hard position right now if he hadn't. But then again, they could've ended up with even more employees to worry about and the damage Jason could've done with his overleveraging could've easily been worse. Luke's head throbbed. They were lucky they were in a bull market right now or it would've been hell.

"Yeah. But it's the pension funds and the unions that are giving us the most trouble right now." Hank shook his head. "I'll go and talk with Betty about opening up the funds."

Luke sighed as he opened his door. At least he knew that he could trust Hank to do as he was told. Hank might not agree with everything Luke did, but he wouldn't defy him the way Jason had.

As it often did, Luke found his mind drifting towards Sam as he got settled in his office. She hadn't even left yet, and he already missed her smile and the sound of her voice. He could just imagine how he'd be months down the line when she was gone.

They'd never really been friends or kept in touch except

through work, so Luke knew he'd be lucky to get the occasional text from her. He briefly wondered if he could use the clients' withdrawal as an excuse to make her stay longer than the two weeks he'd requested before shame filled him. She was doing her best to deal with the hand she'd been given and here he was trying to make it worse for his own selfish needs.

Frightened at how tempted he was to delay buying her out, he got his phone. He wouldn't risk waiting for her to come to the office to tell her that he'd buy her half immediately. He might change his mind by then. Though it might not be best thing to do for the company, a clean break was the best thing he could do for himself and for her. She made him desperate, and it was too easy to see him doing just about anything he could to keep her close to him when the time came to buy her out. With her gone, Harkin would finally have his full attention. He wouldn't be thinking about her constantly and he certainly wouldn't be taking coffee breaks every couple of hours, hoping to catch a glimpse of her.

He frowned as the phone rang. Perhaps it was a good thing Sam had refused him. He didn't exactly have time for a relationship, but he just hadn't been able to stop himself from asking for one. After only one night with Sam, he'd wanted more.

"Luke?"

Pleasure coursed through him at the sound of his name on Sam's lips and he knew that he was making the right decision. With the company the way that it was, he couldn't afford to have any distractions. Blocking out the voice that told him he was making a mistake, he said bluntly, "I'll buy you out. I'll have the paperwork settled before you leave today."

"Wait—are you serious? Thank you, Luke."

"Thank you, too," he said and tried not to think about the relief in her voice. She really wanted out. "I know you could've asked for more."

"You deserve it. I know how much work you've put into the company."

"Jason did as well," he felt compelled to say. Though he was still mad at Jason for overleveraging their clients' money, he knew that there wouldn't have even been a company to worry about if it weren't for Jason. Luke himself would've never had the courage or the resources to start a fund right after college nor would he have had the patience or the connections to court clients.

"If I'd given the stake to Jason's parents, they would've just given it back to me."

She was probably right. Jason's parents loved Sam and it wasn't like they needed the money. With Jason's dad coming from one of the oldest—and richest—families in America and his mom being a trust fund baby, they had more than enough money to last them ten lifetimes.

"Will you send me the list of charities you want to donate to, as well as a preliminary schedule as soon as possible?"

"I—of course. I really wasn't expecting this to be so soon, but thank you. I really appreciate it."

"It's nothing," Luke lied. "I'll have John draft the contract."

His head cleared as he hung up. Sure, he'd just made his

job harder by agreeing to pull even more money from the company, but he knew he could handle the situation. He'd allow a few more investors in, start courting another pension fund or two, and focus on growing the assets they had. It would be challenging, but he'd done it before.

But while his head was clear, his emotions were a mess. And for that, he had no solution, so he shoved those worries aside and focused on work.

* * *

Sam's last day at the company.

Luke's chest tightened he watched Sam put a framed photo into a cardboard box. He couldn't believe she was actually leaving. He guessed some part of him had been hoping for a miracle—that she'd realize she loved her job and decide to stay or that something (anything, really) would come up to make her change her mind, but it had all just been wishful thinking.

Since he didn't know when he would see her again, he took his time to drink in the sight of her. Everything from her soft, dark hair, to those arresting curves her black dress highlighted so well. And it wasn't just the outside he liked. She was even more beautiful on the inside.

Done in true Samantha style, not only was she donating half of the proceeds from the sale of her share in the company, but she'd also started a program using the money she had still invested in Harkin to start a scholarship in Jason's name. Even if Harkin only managed to match the market's return, the money she'd earmarked for the scholarship would be enough to cover the full tuition of five new students every year for a very long time.

Though she would probably say that she was doing the scholarship for Jason's parents, he knew better. She might not be as public about it as Jason had, but she loved to help people.

Realizing he'd stood staring long enough, he rapped softly on her open door. She quickly turned towards him and he forced a smile as he put his hand in his back pocket. "Thank you for walking the guys through on everything."

"It was nothing."

His lips quirked. He'd heard more than one person try to guilt her into staying. Knowing just how close she was to everyone, he couldn't even begin to imagine how hard saying goodbye had been for her. The fact that she was still leaving regardless of how she felt about the people there drove in just how much she wanted to leave.

"Oh. I almost forgot." She turned to get a manila envelope from her desk. "Here are all my keys and credit cards," she said as she handed it to him. "I already cancelled the cards, but I wanted to give them to you just in case you needed them. Most of the keys are labeled, but there are a couple I don't have a clue about." She shrugged. "They just sort of accumulated over the years."

"Thanks," he murmured as he traced the edges of the envelope. He knew that he should be grateful that she was being so considerate to have thought of everything, but instead, all he could think about was how she was giving him even fewer excuses to contact her later.

Shaking the thought off, he asked, "So what will you do

now?" He couldn't imagine her staying idly at home. She was just too much of a hard worker to sit still for too long.

"Well, at first, I thought I'd go back to Anderson. My old manager is now the head of the department and I'm pretty sure he'd hire me."

His heart stopped at her statement and she quickly added, "Don't worry. I realized I couldn't do that when I came in last week."

"I'm sorry, Sam, but you know that you working somewhere else would look really bad for the company, don't you?" The reason they'd given for her leaving was to focus on charity work, so it wasn't as if she could just work at another company.

"I know. But I actually don't know what I'm going to do. I can't see myself joining a charity board. Even before all this stuff with Jason, that was never my scene."

Nor was it his, and he tried not to think about how similar the two of them were. He frowned as a sudden realization occurred.

"Why haven't you ever been given money to manage?" If she'd been anyone else, she would've at least been promoted to junior portfolio manager by now.

"I—" She shrugged. "It just never happened. You know that I just dropped into this industry." She paused as though considering the notion. "You really think I could be a manager?"

He hated the hopefulness in her voice. Had Jason never told her how good she was? Though she didn't have the background the other analysts had, she was just as good as the rest of them. Even better, he thought, though he was probably biased. He loved everything about her—including the reports she'd written. He loved seeing the way her mind worked and loved the fact that he could almost hear her voice when he read her reports.

His fists tightened at the thought of Jason stunting her growth before he cursed himself. It didn't matter what Jason may or may not have done, because Sam was leaving. She was turning her back on Harkin without a single glance back. So instead of saying any of the things he wanted to say, he nodded curtly. "Yeah. I do."

She beamed. "Thank you. Not that I will, but it means a lot that you think I could be one." She shrugged as she put a hand on her box of things. "I just got an apartment on Forty-Ninth and Lex that I'll be moving into this weekend," she said after a moment and he tried not to think about how close she'd be to him. It wasn't as if she were going to pay him any more late night visits.

"You selling the house?"

"Yeah. I figured it would be best. It's a little big for one person."

Anger coursed through him at the knowledge that she was throwing away so many of the things she loved because of Jason—her job, her house… He wanted to tell her that Jason wasn't worth it, but he knew this was just something she had to work out on on her own.

"Do you want to go to dinner tonight?" he asked before he could stop himself. No matter how many times he'd told himself that it would be easier to get over her once she was gone, he was in no hurry to see her leave just yet. If he were being honest with himself, he didn't want to get over her.

Every time he thought about her or that night two weeks ago, he felt as if they belonged together.

She smiled, and his chest suddenly felt lighter. "You have a meeting with Clarence Myers at eight."

Crap. He'd forgotten about that. For a second, he considered blowing off the meeting before guilt crept in. With all the business that they'd lost, he couldn't afford to offend any more clients. "Well, some other time then."

"Sure," she answered without giving an alternative and he knew that she was just being polite. She didn't actually intend on seeing him.

Disappointment settled into his stomach before he cursed himself. What had he been expecting after she'd already turned him down? Instead of wasting time, hoping for the impossible, he should be preparing for his meeting.

With that thought in mind, he took a step back towards the door. "Okay, well, I guess I'll see you around."

CHAPTER TEN

Relief coursed through Sam as she watched her chauffeur help the charity workers load the last of Jason's cars into a truck a week later. *The garage was finally empty.*

Jim, one of the charity workers, approached her when they were done. "Thanks again, Mrs. Collins. We really appreciate this."

"It's no problem. I'm glad the cars can be of use." She'd just wanted everything gone so that she could list the house already.

What had once been her dream home now felt like a representation of all her failed dreams. The room that she'd planned on being the baby's room had been torn down and was now part of a theater Jason had built. The space she'd intended to be the children's playroom had been converted into Jason's home office. Hell, even the area in the backyard where she'd wanted to put a slide and a jungle gym in had been cemented over to put in a gazebo for when they entertained.

And though she'd gotten to pick the paint color and other decorative touches every time they remodeled, it had always been Jason's idea to remodel in the first place. The only thing that she'd wanted and had gotten was the flagstone walkway that trailed along the green for when her parents visited.

Despite the effort, they hadn't visited much because they hadn't felt comfortable at the house. In truth, it had been Jason they hadn't been comfortable with. Because they'd had no problem staying with her after Jason had died. While he'd never been rude to them, he'd never gone out of his way to make them feel at ease, either. He was always talking about places and things they couldn't afford.

And the food!

Her guilt intensified when she remembered one particular instance where her parents had just poked at their food all night. The menu had been in French, so they'd decided to go with the waiter's recommendation, which had turned out to be pig's feet. When she'd confided in Jason afterwards, he'd said that they should've asked the waiter what certain items were or ordered something off the menu. It had seemed so reasonable at the time, but she now realized what a pushover she'd been.

She should've put her foot down when she'd realized that Jason was always picking restaurants her parents hadn't been comfortable eating at, but she hadn't wanted to pick a fight—especially when he'd been the one paying. It had been the same way with all the house renovations as well. She hadn't wanted to make something out of nothing especially when they still had a lot of space.

"It's the biggest donation we've ever gotten," Jim said, drawing her attention back to the present. "Even if we only get half of the cars' value at the auction, it would still be enough to cover all of our expenses for a year."

It was a good thing she hadn't given into temptation and keyed the cars Jason had loved so much after she'd found his phone. She wouldn't have been able to donate any of them or everyone would've seen how she'd truly felt about her husband.

At first, she'd thought about giving the cars to her father-in-law. But considering that Jason had died in a car crash, she hadn't thought it appropriate. Besides, most of the charities she'd chosen to donate to were ones Jason had supported. She was sure his parents would approve.

Some petty part of her didn't want to further support the charities Jason had been involved in, but she knew that it'd be wrong. Just because he'd slept with someone on one charity's board didn't mean that that was his MO. Besides, she couldn't punish a whole charity because of one person's actions, especially when they were doing so much good in the community.

"And judging from the calls we've been getting, this is sure to be our biggest auction ever," Jim continued. "People are already calling for the pre-qualifications."

"That's great. I'm happy that the cars will be put to good use."

"Well, we better get going." He unclipped a paper from his pad and handed it to her. "Here's the receipt for the donation, though I'm sure Connie will be sending an itemized list for the year in February."

"Thank you."

"No. *Thank you*," he said as he hugged the pad to his chest. "You don't know how much this donation means. The children…" As if he were having a hard time finding the words, he shook his head.

She smiled. "Just giving those children a place to hang out after school is more thanks than enough." She didn't know what she and her sister would've done if it hadn't been for community centers like the one this charity ran. Since both of their parents had had full-time jobs, she and her sister had gone to their local community center every day after school. Not only had the center provided them a safe place to stay until their parents picked them up, it had been a second home to them.

As Jim left to join the guys who were talking by the truck, she turned and caught sight of the small stream running through the Japanese garden and suddenly realized how much she was going to miss all of this. It was like having a whole private park in the back of her house. She loved taking walks out here after dinner and enjoyed reading outside when she had the chance.

She frowned when she realized that her backyard was bigger than the park her mom used to take her and her sister to when they'd been younger. Holy, she'd been spoiled. Perhaps moving back to the city would be good for her in more ways than one.

She heard the sound of a car approach and turned to see Nina drive up. "What are you doing here?" Sam asked as soon as Nina got out of the car. Though she was happy to see her friend, it was quite a drive for her—especially with all the traffic.

"I need to borrow a dress. Andrew is coming—"

"Say no more," Sam said as she held her hand up. Though she'd never met Nina's boyfriend, Sam had heard enough about him in recent weeks to make her like him already.

Relief shone in Nina's eyes. "Thanks," she murmured as she hugged her. "You're a lifesaver."

"You should've asked me to take some dresses to my apartment," Sam said as they separated. "It would've saved you the trip."

"I know, but I feel bad enough about always raiding your closet." Nina shrugged. "I would offer you a pick of mine, but it's like a thrift shop compared to yours. Besides, I would've missed these hot studs." She lowered her sunglasses and watched as the men closed the truck. Sam laughed. The woman had no shame.

"They're picking up two of Jason's cars for a charity auction," she explained.

Nina's head whipped around. "Wait—you're giving two of them away?"

"I gave them all away." She didn't want to have anything to do with Jason.

Nina removed her sunglasses. "I hate to break it to you, Sam, but Jason probably lied about the prices of some of those cars. I don't think he ever spent less than half a million on any of them."

"I'm not really thinking about that right now," Sam said,

hoping that she didn't sound like one of those rich wives who never considered the cost of anything. Though Nina was a successful lawyer, one of those cars was easily five times her annual salary.

Nina squeezed her arm. "You're right. I'm sorry."

Damn. She hadn't meant to make her friend feel bad. "It's fine," she quickly said. "And thank you for telling me. I'll keep that in mind when I go through the rest of his stuff," she lied.

"How have you been?" Nina asked as she grabbed her hand.

The look of concern had Sam stiffening. She wasn't up for another round of people trying to console her by saying nice things about Jason. Ever since she'd found out about the cheating and had decided to keep quiet about it, she'd felt as if she were living a lie. People were still offering their condolences and extolling his virtues while all she wanted to do was rail at him for being a lying, cheating ass.

But revealing the truth would hurt Jason's parents and she couldn't do that. They'd always treated her like a member of the family and they'd loved their only son. She would never do anything to taint their memories of him.

"Okay," Sam said. "How's Miranda?" she deflected.

"Don't even get me started on my sister. She's decided to move to L.A., because her boyfriend—her boyfriend of two weeks, mind you—got a job there. She can really be such a—" Nina's grip suddenly tightened, and Sam noticed that her friend was looking at something behind her. She turned to see Jim getting in the truck.

"Hmm… I wonder if they do pickups for books."

"You can check." Sam laughed as she showed her friend the donation receipt with the charity's name and information on the top. "Though I think Andrew might mind."

"Hmph! Sometimes I wonder if he even really cares about me. He barely calls when he's out of town."

Sam's first thought was that he was married before she cursed herself for jumping to conclusions. Just because Jason was a cheater didn't mean that everyone else was as well. Besides, knowing Nina, she was sure that her friend had run every possible search on her boyfriend after their first date. She would've noticed if he was married or if there were photos of him with another woman.

"He's probably busy," Sam finally said. Hopefully, Andrew deserved the benefit of the doubt. Nina didn't deserve to have her heart broken again.

The truck started, and the two men waved as they drove by. Nina inhaled sharply. "Those dimples!"

Sam rolled her eyes. "Didn't you break up with an accountant last year because he had dimples?"

"Because they didn't work on him. Not like Mr. Wowzers over there. Holy." Nina fanned herself. "I can't believe dimples could look so hot on a man."

They were good-looking men, but they had nothing on Luke. They were boyishly handsome where Luke was all man, thin where Luke was all muscle… She inwardly groaned. She had to stop thinking about him. She was in no shape to be in a relationship, and Luke wouldn't be the right man for her even if she were ready.

He had that dark and brooding thing down pat. Along with his wealth, he was someone women would be all over, and she just didn't have it in her to go through all of that again. She didn't want to have to wonder if he was with another woman every time he was stuck at work. And while she knew that Luke wasn't the type to cheat, he didn't do long-term relationships, either. He'd tire of her before she knew it and then, where would she be?

"Come on. Let's go find you a dress," Sam said, hoping to get her mind off the road it was veering towards. She knew that her trusting nature was what had gotten her into this position in the first place, but she hated how cynical she was becoming. "Thanks for all your help, Charles," she said to her chauffeur as they passed by.

"It's no problem, ma'am," he said as he tipped his hat at her.

Sam opened the front door of the house and headed up the marble staircase. A feeling of emptiness seemed to surround the house, and she suddenly realized that the emptiness had always been there. She just hadn't wanted to recognize it.

Even with everything still there, the house felt more like a model than a home. It was devoid of any personal touches and just seemed so clinical. It was almost as if they hadn't lived there… Her throat tightened at the thought that she'd tolerated such a void existence. Worse, she'd convinced herself that she'd been happy.

"Well, this is new," Nina said as they passed a sketch of Central Station. "Wait—did the paintings go to charity, too?"

"No. I loaned them to a museum." It'd never seemed fair that they'd gotten to enjoy all those masterpieces themselves, so she'd loaned them to a museum so that others could enjoy them as well. The museum had been so appreciative that they'd given her some originals done by an up-and-coming local artist.

"That was nice of you," Nina said. "I'm sure a lot of art students will be excited at the opportunity to see the originals."

"I hope so. It had always been Jason's plan to donate the paintings eventually, but then I heard about the Picasso exhibition." She'd consult Jason's mom about what to do with the paintings before the loan period expired. As someone who sat on the board of trustees of a museum, Jessica would know what was best for the paintings instead of just looking at them as a tax deduction the way Jason would've.

They walked into her bedroom and Nina squealed as she ran towards the open closet. "That red dress is gorgeous."

Ten minutes later, Sam watched as Nina twisted and turned in front of the mirror to see if the red dress she was wearing made her butt look big. Sam guessed this was one good thing that had come out of her marriage—getting to loan Nina clothes. Since Jason had never wanted her to wear the same dress twice, she had plenty to share.

"So Jason must've had everything in order for you to be

able to put the house up for sale so quickly," Nina said as she faced the mirror again and patted the dress.

Though she knew that there were women who would've loved to have a rich, dead husband and no one fighting for a share of the pie, Sam would've rather not have gone through it at all. She'd much rather have a marriage like the one her parents had, where they loved each other unconditionally.

Nina looked stricken and quickly turned towards her. "Oh, gosh. I'm really making a muck of this again, aren't I?"

Sam shook her head. "No. You're right. Jason was very thoughtful to have a trust set up so that nothing went into probate." *It was the only right thing he had done.* "I don't even want to think about what would've happened if he hadn't."

She sighed as she looked down at the floor. "He was cheating on me," she admitted in a soft voice.

She hadn't been planning on telling Nina, but she found that she didn't like lying to her closest friend. And in the back of her head, she knew that it wasn't just Jason's parents she was worried about if the truth came out. She was worried about herself as well.

Sure, the media could make her life a living hell, but she was more concerned about what her friends and family would think of her. Many people had thought that she'd been marrying above herself when she'd married Jason. If she admitted that Jason had been cheating on her, they'd probably think that she'd gotten what she deserved for choosing money over love, not knowing or even caring that she'd loved Jason.

"Oh, honey," Nina said as she joined her on the bed and hugged her. "That's why you left the company, wasn't it? And why you're selling the house."

Sam's throat tightened as she nodded. She just wanted a clean break.

"That bastard!" Nina said. "I don't know how you stopped yourself from scratching his cars."

Laughter bubbled inside of Sam, and she was suddenly glad she'd told her friend the truth.

Nina grew serious. "He didn't deserve you. You know that, don't you?"

"I know, but it's just so hard to swallow sometimes." When she'd come back to the house after a week of staying at the hotel, she'd looked at Jason's phone again and had been sick when she'd seen just how many women Jason had been seeing. What's worse was the realization that she'd had to get herself tested. Though she was thankfully clean, she couldn't help but feel as if Jason hadn't cared about her at all.

"There's nothing to think about," Nina said. "There are men who will cheat regardless of who they're with, just because they can."

"I think it's just hard that I can't talk to him about it. It's like I can never get closure." Instead, she was filled with questions. Had he been planning on divorcing her? Or had he been content seeing other people behind her back? Did she or any of those other women actually mean anything to him? Or was his cheating only about his ego? Though the answers didn't really matter in the grand scheme of things, she still wanted to know.

"Sometimes, revenge is better than closure."

Remembering the revenge Nina had gotten on a boyfriend she'd caught cheating on her, Sam smiled. Nina had hired someone to come over to the apartment she and Paul had shared to beat Paul's high score on a video game while he'd been out. Afterwards, she'd simply put her name beside the high-score, gotten her things, and left. Later, she'd sublet her half of the apartment to a co-worker who loved to expound about how violent video games were a threat to society.

"Too bad you already gave all his cars away," Nina continued. "It would've been fun to take a bat to one of them." She snapped her fingers suddenly. "Hey—how about sleeping with a competitor?" she asked as she looked at her. When Sam raised her eyebrows, Nina's shoulders slumped. "Yeah. I didn't think so, either. They're probably all old and ugly anyway." Her head rose. "Hey—how about going to a club? We haven't done that in ages."

"Because we're getting too old for clubbing," Sam said wryly. She couldn't even remember the last time she'd gone to a club.

"That's a load of bull. You know that we can never be too old for clubbing."

Sam smiled. "Thanks for the offer, but I still have a lot to do here." She didn't want to have to make any more trips to the house than she had to. "Let's go out next week, so I can hear all about your date with Andrew."

Nina's thirst for revenge served as a reminder that Sam was the injured party. She often forgot that and found herself thinking about all the things she'd done wrong. Her parents had raised her to take responsibility for her actions and decisions, and that's exactly what she'd been doing. In spades. But Nina had reminded her that Jason had treated her love and loyalty as though it'd been nothing and Sam would do well to remember that.

"I'm sure I'll be calling you sooner than that, but okay. That works. Now, about that green dress…"

CHAPTER ELEVEN

Luke let his shoulders relax as he wrapped up the weekly meeting between the portfolio managers and the analysts. Thankfully, today's meeting had gone better than the ones from previous weeks. The fresh influx of money had really boosted the people's morale.

"I should have the report sent to you by five o'clock," Ross told him.

"I appreciate it," Luke said as he stood. He glanced around and saw that most of the people had already left the meeting room. In the five weeks since Sam had left, they'd been able to pull in a few new investors and had managed to mitigate more of the risk Jason's overleveraging had caused. The company still wasn't on the stable ground Luke preferred, but things were definitely looking better. He opened the glass door to let Ross exit first.

Chris approached him as he was about to follow. "You're not seriously going to give Sam's office to Dean, are you?" the junior manager asked, and Luke sighed. There was a time when people had cornered him to ask for a promotion or for more money to manage, but nowadays, all people seemed to want was either Jason's or Sam's office.

"I haven't decided what I'm going to do with Sam's and Jason's offices yet," he answered. Though he knew they weren't coming back, it just didn't feel right to give either of their offices away. To him, the rooms would always be theirs.

And deep down, he was still hoping Sam would come back. He understood her reasons for leaving, but he also knew how much she loved working at the company. She'd miss it sooner or later and when she did, he wanted to be ready.

"I want Sam's office," Chris announced and leveled a stare at him. "You know that I deserve it."

"What's wrong with yours?" He didn't know the exact size, but it was possible Chris's office was bigger than Sam's.

"It doesn't have a view of Bryant Park."

Luke shook his head unbelievingly. The go-get-them attitude was a trait all their managers had, and while it made them good at their jobs, it could be downright annoying sometimes.

"I'm going back to work, and I suggest you do the same."

Without waiting for the man to respond, Luke left the meeting room.

As he sat behind his desk a minute later, Luke realized that Jason would've handled the situation differently. Jason would have still said no, but would've done so in that charming way of his that always left the other person smiling, feeling as if he'd won. Luke was just thinking about how he could've handled Chris's request differently when his phone rang, interrupting his musings.

He looked at the screen. *Sam.* He quickly swiped the phone's screen and tried to ignore the frantic beating of his pulse. He knew that some of the employees still asked her questions sometimes, but he hadn't heard from her personally since she'd left, and he'd missed her.

Are you free for lunch on Saturday?

Had she changed her mind about giving him a chance? Hope leaped inside of him.

Yeah. Is everything okay?

He wouldn't get ahead of himself. After weeks of not seeing her, he'd realized that he wanted her in his life in any way that he could get. He wouldn't ruin it by rushing her into something she wasn't ready for. Even if it was just friendship, he'd force himself to accept that.

Things are great. I just wanted to see if you were available for lunch.

I am. I can pick you up at eleven.

Awesome! See you soon!

Smiling, he put away his phone. The more realistic side of him knew not to get his hopes up. She hadn't been interested in a relationship a few weeks ago and it was unlikely that she'd changed her mind so soon. But at the same time, he couldn't stop himself from hoping that she had and he knew that Saturday couldn't come soon enough.

* * *

Is this inappropriate for a lunch date with a friend?

Sam considered the sexy blue dress before rejecting it. It was too short. Definitely not appropriate. She put the dress back on the rack and groaned when she'd realized that she'd already rejected a third of her dresses. This was insane. She'd eaten with Luke before. Why was she suddenly so self-conscious about this lunch?

Because they'd slept together. And he'd been constantly on her mind.

Was he a friend, or something more? If she were completely honest with herself, she was attracted to Luke and wouldn't mind exploring a relationship with him. But, at the same time, she knew that she still wasn't in the best frame of mind for a relationship. Though she was feeling steadier and more like herself, the bitterness and hurt were still there and messed with her sometimes.

And on the other side of her dilemma was the knowledge that she could really use a friend like Luke. After being surrounded by people who were only nice to her because they wanted something, it was freeing to be with someone who didn't have a secret agenda, who was just genuinely nice.

Damn. She hoped she hadn't messed things up with him. She'd invited him to lunch to get a sense of where they were and to try to build on the burgeoning friendship between them.

Because no matter what she'd always told herself about him, he really was one of the good guys. She'd never once seen him take advantage of the people and businesses who came to him for help and he donated for the simple reason of donating instead of trying to maximize his tax deductions or to boost his PR.

Frustrated at her continued wardrobe debate and knowing that she was making something out of nothing, she took out the first pair of jeans she saw as well as the blouse closest to her. This was what happened when she didn't work. She got fussy about the silliest things.

She was just putting on lipstick a few minutes later when the doorbell rang. Despite the butterflies raging inside of her, she forced herself to calmly put the lipstick down and checked herself at the mirror one last time before making her way towards the living room.

Her heart skipped a beat when she saw Luke on the small video screen by the door. He was so handsome. The memory of how his stubbled jaw felt against her skin sent shivers down her spine. She imagined touching it again, running her fingers along his…

Get it together, Sam.

Shaking away her lustful thoughts, she opened the door and was struck by how dark his eyes were. Her throat tightened. "Hey. Um… Let me just get my purse."

"I brought you some cookies," he said as he handed her a bag. It was only then that she noticed the familiar brown bag he was holding. She'd been so focused on him that she hadn't noticed anything else.

"Oh. Thank you." The bag was still warm and she couldn't help but be touched. Not only had he remembered how much she loved the cookies from Nadine's, he'd gone out of his way to get them.

"Let me just set these down."

She let go of the door to put the cookies on the table by her couch. When she turned back, she saw that Luke had entered and was looking around her living room. She could just imagine how small it must seem to him. Though her apartment was spacious and definitely big by New York standards, it was a far cry from his grand apartment, whose living room alone was almost as big as her whole apartment.

And sure, she could've gotten a place like his, but she hadn't wanted to use up more of Jason's money than she had to. At least on herself. She had no problem splurging on things for her family. Though she knew nothing could make up for the way she'd practically abandoned them during her marriage, she wanted to try.

"Nice place you got here," Luke finally said.

Hearing the sincerity in his voice, she looked around the room she'd designed and smiled.

"Thanks. I like it."

It wasn't fancy, but everything from the couch to the dining room table was all her. She'd even assembled the bookshelf by herself.

"Any suggestions on where to eat?" Luke asked.

Because he hadn't turned his nose down at her apartment or said that he had a designer he could recommend, as Jason surely would've, impulse took her. "I'm not sure if you know about it, but there's this restaurant in the Village called Flanigan's."

"I know it."

"Really?" It was a restaurant known for its cheap food. She couldn't imagine Luke eating in a place like that.

He shrugged. "It was one of the few places I could actually afford in college."

"Me, too. I forgot that we went to the same college." And apparently had had the same money problems. She took her coat from the coat rack. "I haven't been there in ages. I know I'm probably imagining the food's better than it really is, but I still want to go."

"I know what you mean. I used to love their sandwiches."

"I tried bringing it to the house once," she said as she locked her door. There were times she was just so fed up with having to wonder if something was organic, free range, or whole-wheat. Sometimes, she just wanted something delicious even if it was bad for her. "But it just isn't the same as when it's hot."

He laughed as they made their way towards the elevator. "I'm sure Jason would've loved that."

"I did it while he was away," she admitted. "I thought I was so smart. Since Jason didn't want me eating there anymore, I went when he was out with a client."

Luke frowned. "He dictated where you ate?"

"Yeah. He didn't want his wife to be seen at what's basically a dive." She'd been angry at him but had tried to look at it from his point of view. He was courting clients that were worth millions of dollars and his wife was going to a bar for dinner? Though she still hadn't completely agreed with it, she'd eventually given in. And without her noticing, her acquiescence had gradually spread to other things. Eventually, she'd stopped going to any restaurant or place that didn't fit his criteria. It had been the same way with her clothes and friends.

"It doesn't surprise me," Luke said. "He had me get a new wardrobe, so that I would look presentable enough when we met prospective clients."

Her eyebrows rose as they continued walking. "I can't imagine anyone—even Jason—telling you what to do."

"In a way, I wanted it. I wanted to fit in with the rich crowd. After being poor for most of my life, it was like a dream come true. It'd felt as if I'd finally made it." He shrugged. "But it got old pretty fast and I doubled down on the investing side of things."

"How did you get interested in investing?" she asked as they arrived at the elevators and she pressed the down button. She knew all about how he and Jason had met at Brown and Hale, and had started the fund, but she barely knew anything about Luke's life beforehand.

"Growing up, I'd always heard about the stock market on the news, but I never really thought about it until a food manufacturer opened up a factory nearby when I was a sophomore in high school. They were moving there from a smaller location across town and I realized that business must be improving for them to get a bigger space. I had a little money saved from working at an auto shop after school and bought some of the company's stocks." He grinned at her as they entered the elevator. "I was very simplistic back then. I didn't make any calls or even open up an annual report."

She laughed. "And I thought my sister and I were enterprising for our age when we graded papers for concert money."

"You were. I can't imagine how many teenagers would do that." He gave her an admiring look. "How about you? How did you get interested in accounting?"

"My story isn't anywhere as interesting as yours," she said and began telling him about how she'd gravitated towards it simply because she'd been good at math and horrible at just about every other subject.

Their conversation eased the worst of her fears. For a man who didn't make small talk, Luke was chatting easily with her. Surely that meant she hadn't screwed up too much by sleeping with him, didn't it?

* * *

Sam walked into the familiar restaurant and blinked when she saw the faded leather booths and the suspiciously dark walls. *Had it always been this dark in here?*

No. It couldn't have been. Flanigan's had been one of her favorite haunts to do her homework when she'd been in college. She wouldn't have chosen it if it had been this dark, no matter how good their beef sandwiches were. How would she have even seen her homework?

It was probably just because they'd come during the day that made things seem different. Since she'd had classes and work during the day, she'd always come here at night. The difference in time would also explain why the place wasn't wall-to-wall packed the way it could be some nights, though it was still crowded enough. Knowing that it was useless, she scanned the place for an empty table—or even, an empty chair.

"Sorry," she said when her search came out dry. "I wasn't expecting it to be so full at this time of day. Do you just want to order and eat outside?"

"Sure."

As they made their way through the crowd, Sam couldn't help but notice the glances that came their way. Or, to be precise, Luke's way. She had to admit that even if they didn't know who he was, he was still a sight to behold. Whether he was in a suit or khakis, there was just something about him that was innately sexy. Knowing that she didn't even want to go there, she forced the thought out of her head and joined the end of the line.

She guessed this was another example of how Luke was different than Jason. He was willing to line up. Jason, on the other hand, usually just passed the line and went straight towards the front desk. He didn't even have to have a reservation. He'd be given a table the moment the maître d' saw him. Sam had used to chide Jason for not bothering to make reservations, but after he'd made and missed a couple, she'd let the issue go. Knowing how tacky Jason would find the menu attached on the wall, she smiled. Her smile grew even larger when she realized that it hadn't changed.

"What are you getting?" Luke asked as he leaned towards her.

"The tri-tip," she responded as she looked up to meet his eyes. "You?"

"The brisket."

Mmm. The brisket here was good, too. Luke laughed

when he saw her face. "Do you want to split the sandwiches?"

"No, thanks." It was going to be hard enough not getting sauce on their clothes while they ate on a bench. She didn't even want to think about how much harder it would be to cut the sandwiches without the sauce exploding everywhere. Those babies were wrapped tight.

"Too bad. I was looking forward to the tri-tip."

And she really wanted the brisket. "We'd probably get sauce all over our clothes," she warned.

"I don't mind."

She beamed. Jason would've never have allowed a single spot to mar his clothes if he could prevent it and she found that she liked the idea of getting a little messy with Luke. In more ways than one. "Okay then, but don't say I didn't warn you."

After they'd reached the front of the line and placed their order, Sam opened her bag to grab her wallet.

"Let me," Luke said as he got his own wallet out.

Sam frowned as she handed her credit card to the cashier. "I was the one who invited."

"It's a guy thing. Humor me, okay?"

"That's insane. I even got to pick the restaurant." When the cashier still didn't take her card, she turned towards him, silently imploring him with her eyes. After what seemed like forever, he made a move towards her before he stopped and looked at Luke, who was holding out a card as well. She inwardly groaned. If Luke gave him that hard stare of his, there was no way the man would take her card. Hell. Even she hated to be at the receiving end of *that* stare.

"Are we really arguing about who's going to pay for an eight-dollar sandwich?" Luke asked.

The absurdity of the question made her laugh out loud. Feeling the cashier's gaze on her, she quickly covered her laugh with a cough. Nope. It definitely wasn't the time to suddenly grow a conscience about who paid for meals.

But she'd wanted to feel like her own person. Having her own apartment and doing things herself these past few weeks had been unbelievably freeing, and she hadn't wanted to stop. But she knew when to pick her battles.

"Fine." She put the card back in her bag. "Thank you."

Luke shook his head, murmuring something about crazy women and she figured he was right. It wasn't unusual for their meals to be over a thousand dollars when the three of them had gone out to eat and she was fighting over a sixteen dollar one?

"I haven't done this in a while," she admitted as they stepped to the side to wait for their order.

"What? Go on a date?"

Her heart stopped at the thought of this being a real date. She'd often wondered what would've happened if she hadn't rejected his offer to explore a relationship with him. Sure, it wouldn't have lasted for very long, but it would have been thrilling for however long it did. She glanced at him and quickly cursed herself when she saw his questioning stare. Of course, he didn't mean it in *that* way. He just meant date in the going out sort of way.

"No. I meant to go out and eat with a friend," she clarified. Things were always so busy at the office, and Jason had always had a full schedule. "I've forgotten how this works. Nina and I always take turns and most of those meals with Jason were billed to the company unless it was a special occasion." Her lips quirked. "Is it really eight dollars?"

"Beats me."

She laughed. "When's the last time you looked at the prices on a menu?"

"Last week."

Her eyebrows rose and he shrugged.

"Adam was taking too long to decide on what to order. I thought it would be rude to take out my phone."

She'd never seen him take out his phone those times they'd gone to eat, and she suddenly realized how strange that was. He was always on top of things business-wise and it would've made sense for someone like him to be glued to his phone when he wasn't physically at the office. But he wasn't like that. He always gave people his full attention.

"I haven't looked at the prices on a menu in a long time," she admitted. It was crazy. Growing up, she'd always had to look at prices to make sure that she could afford whatever it was that she wanted. There were even times she hadn't been able to go to certain restaurants because she hadn't been able to afford them. Now she could go anywhere she wanted, anytime she wanted.

It was insane. She poured through financials, looking for even the slightest discrepancies, almost to the penny, and she couldn't even be bothered to check the price of the meal she was getting?

"It's not always about the price," Luke pointed out. "I

doubt you'd stop buying the chocolate at Gerard if they increased their prices tenfold."

"How did you know I like Gerard?" He'd known that she liked the cookies at Nadine's as well.

"You forget that we've worked together. There were times I'd walk by your office and see you eating a chocolate from a familiar silver-colored box."

"I like to reward myself with chocolate."

Dark eyebrows rose. "At eight in the morning?"

She shrugged. "It's a reward for waking up early." He laughed, and she continued, "You don't know what it's like with the commute. Sometimes, I just wanted to ask Charles to turn the car around." Even being spoiled with a private driver didn't change the frustration when you were stuck in traffic.

She poked him after he gave her a knowing smile. "Just wait. One day, you'll be the one living in the suburbs and you'll understand how it feels." Though why the thought of him with another woman made her stomach turn, she didn't want to examine too closely.

Luke grinned at the same time someone called their number. "I don't think we have to worry about that happening unless you've finally decided to take me out of my misery and marry me."

She laughed as she followed him towards the counter. She never knew he could be such a joker.

Once they'd gotten their food and drinks, they went outside and found an empty bench at a park nearby. As if a little extra distance between them would help with the attraction she was battling, she set the bag down between them. He followed suit and placed their bottles of water down as well. She guessed that even though they were both willing to eat the restaurant's food, they hadn't wanted to test the cleanliness of the fountain machine.

The familiar smell of the sandwiches beckoned her as she opened the bag. She was finally going to find out whether or not she'd hyped up the sandwich in her head. She opened the sandwiches then carefully cut them each in half, trying not to let too much sauce ooze out. She wrapped one in a napkin then handed it to Luke. "Good luck."

It was a good thing he wasn't wearing one of his suits or she'd feel awful if anything got stained. She wrapped another napkin around the remaining half, then took a bite, and moaned. She'd forgotten how good their barbecue sauce was. The sandwich might not be organic, free range, or even whole-wheat, but, oh, how she'd missed it. She took another bite, then another.

After a while, she realized that she hadn't heard anything from Luke. She wiped her mouth and turned to find him looking at her with the oddest expression. Her throat tightened. She doubted the glamorous women he dated brought him to rundown bars and ate messy sandwiches. And though she knew that she was overthinking things, she couldn't help but feel self-conscious. She was about to ask him why he wasn't eating when he moved to brush his thumb against her mouth. Her heartbeat quickened, and she intercepted him to wipe her mouth with a napkin.

"You're not eating," she murmured.

He looked like he was about to say something before he shook his head. "I was just thinking about something."

He lifted his sandwich and some sauce dropped onto his khakis. Her cheeks flushed as she set her sandwich down. "I'm sorry. I should've wrapped these better." She opened her bag and got a baby wipe before moving closer towards him. Pulling the fabric of his pants, she wiped the sauce off. Then she folded the wipe and dabbed the spot, hoping to remove the stain.

After a few dabs, he made a sound and took a hold of her hand, sending electric shivers up her arm. "I'll do it. Thank you."

Her cheeks flushed as she suddenly realized how close she'd been to his penis. "Of course," she said as she quickly released the wipe.

As he worked the stain, she took a drink from her water bottle and tried her best not to look at him. With the way her mind seemed to be working lately, she was sure she was going to look at something she had no business looking at.

"There," he said a moment later.

She glanced down and breathed a sigh of relief when she saw that the stain was almost gone. "At least it looks better," she said. "Hopefully, Maria won't kill me when she sees it." His housekeeper and cook kept a tight ship.

He scoffed. "Maria adores you. If anything, she'd probably blame me." He wrapped another napkin around the sandwich and as he brought it to his mouth, she couldn't help but notice how big his hands were.

She forced herself to look away and felt her throat go dry as she watched the muscles in his neck work. How could she find him eating sexy? Forcing her attention back to her own sandwich, she inwardly cursed herself. She'd invited him to lunch to try to salvage what she'd hoped was the beginning of a new friendship, but instead of doing that, she was ogling him as if he were her dessert. Insane. She was definitely insane.

* * *

"Thanks for lunch," Sam said as they got out of the elevator in her apartment building a few hours later. Luke looked up from her perfectly shaped ass to spy her getting her key from her bag and breathed a sigh of relief. Thank goodness she hadn't caught him looking at her. He really shouldn't have even been looking at her ass, but holy, did her jeans fit her well.

"It was nothing," he murmured as he burrowed his hands into his pockets.

Sam laughed as she opened her door. "Your nothing was the most fun I've had in ages."

He smiled and tried not to let that get into his head. She was probably bored from staying home most of the time. "I had fun, too." After they'd eaten, they'd taken a walk around the university and something about it had just felt right. He hadn't wanted the day to end. "Let me know if you ever need anything at the office to help with your investing."

She'd mentioned she'd started trading and had credited it to him. He couldn't help but be happy that not only was she doing something she loved, but that she'd thought highly enough of him to listen to his idea. Though it was wasn't anywhere near as much as he'd been thinking about her, it was something.

"Thanks. I appreciate it." She tapped her keys against her hand. "So...maybe we'll do this again sometime?" Her smile made his chest do all kinds of crazy things and he suddenly realized that they were alone. His gaze dropped to her lips and he had to tamp down the urge to take her in his arms and kiss her. All he had to do was take a step forward and he'd get to taste those sweet lips he'd been looking at all day.

"I'll text you." He took a step back, putting some distance between her and his wild urges. He would undoubtedly do something extremely stupid if he stayed with her a second longer. She was just too tempting for his own good. He'd thought he could keep his feelings at bay, but all through lunch, he'd found himself watching for signs that she'd wanted to be more than friends. Unfortunately, there'd been none. And though he'd been expecting that, the disappointment still hurt.

"Sure."

His chest ached at the realization that he was going to have to limit the time he spent with her. He couldn't accept any more lunch invitations from her and he most definitely shouldn't text her. He'd never get over her if he did.

"I should get going," he said as he tilted his head down the hallway. "I still have some work to catch up on. It was good seeing you again."

"Yeah. You, too."

He smiled grimly and left.

* * *

Hey, do you want to go out on Saturday?

Luke's chest tightened as he looked at Sam's text. It had been almost two weeks since they'd gone out to lunch together and while he loved the fact that she'd enjoyed it so much that she wanted to do it again, he couldn't put himself through it all again. He'd always find himself wanting more than she could give him and that wouldn't be fair to either of them.

And yet, he was hesitant to refuse.

A year ago, he would've jumped at the opportunity to spend more time with her. It hadn't mattered that she was married and all that he could hope for was friendship. He would've taken anything he could get. But with Jason no longer between them, being friends no longer cut it. He wanted *everything*.

And since she couldn't give him what he wanted, he had to stop fooling himself. He had to cut her loose. He'd never get over her if he didn't.

Disappointment settled low in his belly, but he knew it was the right thing to do. He'd never gotten over her when she'd been married to Jason and now that she was single, it was going to be downright impossible.

I'm sorry, Sam. I'm busy.

No matter how much it hurt, he wouldn't push his feelings on her. What would be the point? She already knew how he felt and she wasn't interested.

When it became clear that he wasn't going to expand, she replied a minute later.

That's okay. Hope you have a good weekend!

Yeah, right. As if he could have a good weekend without her. He'd doubled his workload to help keep his mind off her, but it hadn't worked. He still thought of her constantly.

He set his phone down and ran a hand over his face as he looked at it. He hated knowing that he might've hurt her with his rejection, but distancing himself was his only hope to get over her.

CHAPTER TWELVE

Luke was walking towards his office a month later when Hank joined him.

"Peter's working at Blue Asset Management," his COO said as he handed him a printout.

"Good for him," Luke answered instinctively without stopping. Peter hadn't been happy when Luke had chosen George to lead Jason's fund over him, but George had truly been the better choice. Not only was he the stronger analyst, but he was also a better team player. He wasn't afraid to share what he knew, and he was always willing to listen when someone disagreed with him. Peter, on the other hand, was a one-man island. He always kept things to himself and never bothered to give anyone with an opposing view the time of day—especially if they were junior staff.

"Not good," Hank said as he nodded at the paper he'd given him. "Read the article."

Sighing, Luke glanced at the article. *Top Harkin Executive Joins Blue Asset Management*

Shit.

He tried to think about some of the clients Peter had handled and cursed again when he realized how big some of those accounts were. This was not what he needed right now.

"At least we know we saved ourselves from making a huge mistake by promoting George," he said, trying to lighten the situation. "Peter didn't even have the balls to start his own fund."

Hank didn't smile. "Continue reading," he said grimly.

Luke did and felt a sense of foreboding when he saw Sam's name. The article insinuated that Sam had left because she hadn't agreed with the direction he was steering the company. Along with Peter leaving, the paper was making it seem as if people were jumping ship.

Fuck.

He should've known it was too early to buy her out.

He looked at Hank. "What's your plan?"

"Oh, now you want to listen to me."

Luke sighed. Hank was still on his case for not agreeing to meet with the clients sooner even though he'd taken great pains to remedy that. "Am I going to hear about this forever?"

Hank grinned. "Pretty much. You're almost never wrong. I might as well enjoy this while I can."

Luke shook his head. "You do have a plan, don't you?" His COO always had a plan.

"I do, but you're not going to like it," Hank warned as they stepped into an empty hallway. "It would be best if you and Sam attended some kind of gala or ball together, so that everyone can see that there's no bad blood between you."

Luke's heart leapt at the chance of seeing Sam again. He hadn't called or texted her since the last time she'd invited him to lunch, but she'd been on his mind constantly. He kept wondering where she was, what she was doing, who she was with…

"You know how the press is," Hank continued. "If they don't see certain people together in a while, they hint at frictions or feuds." Luke didn't bother to mention that they had gone out together in public. The press just hadn't seen them. "Look, I know how much you hate these things, but it's a lot better than Sam just issuing some kind of a statement."

Luke nodded. "I'll see what I can do. The Children's Society gala is coming up soon. I'll ask her if she has a date yet."

"Really? That's it?" Hank asked incredulously. "You're not going to tell me that galas are a waste of time? That you'd rather swim with sharks than be interviewed by a bunch of good-for-nothing reporters?"

Luke's lips twitched. Though he did hate these kinds of things, he'd endure a lot more just to have an excuse to see Sam again. He hadn't seen her in weeks, and frankly, he missed her so much that it hurt.

"No. I'm not going to argue with you," Luke murmured. "It's a good plan. Besides, I now know what happens when

I don't listen to you. How're Barbara and the kids doing, by the way?"

Hank froze, and Luke knew that he'd caught the man off guard. Ever since he'd realized that the employees weren't comfortable with him, Luke had been making an effort to talk with them more. But he guessed his efforts weren't enough if people were still surprised when he asked about them and their families.

"They're fine," Hank said after a moment. "Barbara and I were worried about how Nathan would take another kid in the family, but he's already acting like a big brother. Yesterday, he told me that I had to change his baby brother's diaper, because it was smelly."

Luke laughed. He remembered when he'd had to change his sister's diapers and was grateful that Anna had grown up quickly. "How old is Nathan?"

"He'll be three next month," Hank said, surprising him. That meant Nathan had been born after Hank had started working at the company and yet, Luke hadn't known about the child until recently.

Though Sam had said that Hank wasn't one of those people who mentioned his kid in every conversation, having a kid seemed like something that should've come up at least once over the seven years that they'd worked together, and he couldn't help but wonder what else he didn't know.

Hank shook his head. "Sometimes it's hard to believe how fast time flies."

"He'll be breaking hearts in no time."

"I don't even want to think about first grade."

Though Luke knew nothing about children, it was nice to see a parent enjoy being a parent.

He nodded at Hank. "Thanks for letting me know about the article. I'll go ahead and call Sam."

Excitement pulsed through him as he walked away and reached for his cell phone. It'd been weeks since he'd heard Sam's voice, and he was starved. Like a junkie, he was hooked on her, and he suddenly realized that it had been futile to stay away from her. He'd just ended up missing her more.

The phone rang in his ear and he smiled. In a little more than a week, he'd have Sam in his arms once again.

* * *

"You should've let me get this one, Sam. You're already treating me to a dinner and a show."

Her sister's words needled at Sam. The fact that Cindy thought going to a show together was a treat was proof of just how much Sam had allowed them to grow apart over these past few years. What's worse was that her mom had specifically asked her to keep an eye on Cindy when she'd first moved into the city. And instead of doing that, Sam had practically left her sister to her own devices. Even though Cindy had a good head on her shoulders, Sam should've still made the effort to take her sister out once in a while. But she'd been so caught up in Jason's world that she'd dropped the ball on being a big sister. Big time.

"It's nothing," Sam murmured as she signed her name on the pad.

"But I *want* to pay sometimes. You're always doing and buying things for me."

Sam laughed as she got their lattes and scanned the crowded café for an empty table.

"Now you know that's not true," she said and breathed a sigh of relief when she spotted an empty table near the back.

"It is," her sister argued as she trailed after her. "You paid for my graduate school."

"Only what was left after the scholarships," Sam said as she carefully placed the two lattes on the table and sat while Cindy set down the pastries.

"You got me my dream espresso maker and even sent me and Hailey on a luxury cruise."

"That was for your graduation—that I missed by the way." She'd accompanied Jason to a power breakfast that had taken longer than expected. Knowing just how tight the scheduling had been, she really shouldn't have gone to the breakfast, but Jason had assured her that she wouldn't miss the graduation.

Cindy waved her off. "What could you do? You were busy. Besides, you made it to the celebration dinner and that's the important thing."

Her sister's words only deepened her guilt. Sam had been such a nonexistent sister that by the time graduation had come, Cindy had pretty much known not to expect anything from her. Because how on earth could a dinner be the important part of a graduation?

Sam remembered the way they used to talk for hours

when she'd moved out for college. They'd been so close then and now, she was lucky if they talked once a week.

Sam leaned towards her sister. "The thing is I know that I've been a pretty shitty sister these past few years and I want to make up for it."

Now that she could look at her life with a clear view, she realized how much she'd let her relationship with Jason cloud over her responsibility to her friends and family—how much she'd let herself get caught up in his world and she wasn't proud of it.

Cindy shook her head. "You're being too hard on yourself. You were always there when it mattered."

Sam wasn't quite sure of that, but she was going to be a better sister from now on—she wouldn't just be a sister when it was appropriate for *her*.

"Wait. Is this what tonight is all about? Making things up to me?"

"I also wanted to watch the musical," Sam lied, and Cindy laughed.

"I should've known something was up when you invited me. I know how much you hate musicals, but I couldn't stop myself. I've been wanting to see this for ages and the tickets are *so* expensive."

Sam guessed that that was another good thing that came out of her marriage. She got to buy expensive Broadway tickets to bribe her sister into spending time with her. Sam took a sip of her latte and sighed. This was really good. "What's the name of this café again?"

"Deux Pains," Cindy answered. "Why?"

Sam shook her head as she got her phone and quickly made a note in it. "I was just wondering if it's a public company or not." She shrugged as she put her phone in her bag. "It's not just the location that has this place so crowded," she said as she scanned the tables, taking in the eclectic crowd. The café catered to everyone from students to businessmen. "The coffee—and I assume the food as well—is really good." It was companies like this that had the potential to grow.

"You just can't stop it, can you?" Cindy said, laughing. "Even when you're eating, you're working."

"Sorry. I've started investing a little bit." Remembering that her sister had met Luke a few times, she suddenly wondered what her sister thought of him before she quickly shook the thought off. It didn't matter what Cindy thought of Luke, because Sam wasn't seeing Luke.

"Oh! That's awesome! Can I start telling people about you?"

"I'm sorry. What?"

"About your investing," Cindy clarified. "People—you know, like the Jacksons—are always asking about investing with Harkin, but since I know they don't meet the requirements for the hedge fund, I just tell them that it's closed to new clients."

Sam smiled at her sister's thoughtfulness. She'd been telling the truth without hurting anyone's feelings. The SEC had strict rules about who could invest in hedge funds, taking into account people's net worth and salaries. They wanted to make sure that the investors knew and could handle the risks they were taking. And though Sam knew that what her parents' neighbors were willing to invest wasn't small to them, she very much doubted that the retired couple would meet the SEC's requirements.

"Then they ask me for stock tips, which I know absolutely nothing about." Cindy shrugged as she gestured towards her. "It would be great if I could point them to you."

"I can't. I mean, I've barely been doing this for a month." Even Luke and Jason had invested their own money for a couple years before they'd started managing other people's money.

But the idea was definitely intriguing. She loved the thought of helping a hard-working family grow their savings instead of helping the rich clientele hedge funds catered to get richer.

"But isn't that what you did at Harkin?"

"I researched companies, but I never actually handled the buying and selling part."

"I figure that should be the easy part."

"I'll think about it," she hedged. It was one thing to trade her own money to see if she could make a decent income and quite another to handle someone else's life savings. She'd have to take a much more conservative route than the one she'd taken for herself if she decided to do it. Though her portfolio was mostly filled with stable companies, she also had a few wild cards in there as well, which had big potential upsides and big potential downsides.

She'd have to see how her investments fared and make sure that she really wanted to do this before she agreed to handle anyone's money. "But in the meantime, tell them to invest in index funds." Historically, it was the best way to go. Only the best of the best could beat the market year after year.

"Believe me, I have, but you know how people are."

She nodded. "I know. People are always out to make the quickest—" She was interrupted by the ringing of her phone and sighed. It had better not be another reporter who'd gotten hold of her new number or there'd be hell to pay.

She got her phone and felt her heart skip a beat when she saw Luke's name. Though he'd been on her mind constantly, they hadn't actually spoken since he'd brushed off her invitation to lunch. The weird thing was, she'd actually thought that he'd had a good time when they'd gone out, but she'd obviously thought wrong.

"Aren't you going to answer it?" Cindy asked.

Sam knew she was being a coward, but she hated how twisted up he made her. She was supposed to be getting over men and instead, it seemed as if she'd fallen for the next guy she'd seen.

"I—of course." It could be something at the office or a problem with one of the donations. "I'm sorry," she murmured to her sister as she swiped her phone. "It's Luke."

Cindy waved her off. "Of course."

Smiling her thanks, Sam pressed the phone to her ear and answered. "Hi, Luke."

"Hey, Sam. Do you have a date for the Children's Society gala?" he asked without preamble and she couldn't help but smile. It was so him. He always went straight down to business without wasting time on small talk.

"No." She actually didn't want to go. But since a big reason for that was because she didn't want to run into one of the women Jason had been having an affair with, she was forcing herself to go. Not that she intended to confront Carla. She just needed to prove to herself that she wasn't hiding. Besides, her in-laws expected her to be there. There was going to be some kind of tribute for Jason.

"Do you want to go together?"

Her heart sped at the thought of seeing Luke again before she frowned. "But you hate these things." The only reason he'd gone in the past was because Jason had twisted his arm. Now that Jason was gone, she figured he'd burn all his tuxes.

"I do, but they have that tribute thing for Jason," he said.

Of course. It had been crazy to think that his invitation had anything to do with her. He'd made it more than clear that he had no interest in being friends with her.

There was a brief pause before he added, "And I was hoping to set down a rumor that there's some friction between us."

"What rumor?"

"That you left because you didn't agree with the way I was managing the company. There was an article in the *Times.*"

Guilt bit her at the knowledge that he wouldn't have had this problem if she'd stayed at Harkin. "I'm so sorry, Luke." She shouldn't have pressed to leave, but she'd been desperate.

"Excuse me," a voice interrupted. "Can I take this chair?"

Sam looked up to see a man in a suit pointing at the chair beside her. Cindy put down the croissant she was eating and answered, "Yes" the same time Luke asked, "Who's that?"

A thrill ran down Sam's spine. Was it just her or did he sound jealous?

The thought had barely registered before she cursed herself. She shouldn't enjoy the thought of him being jealous, because there was no them. Why couldn't she seem to get that through that thick head of hers?

"It's just a guy from another table," she said off-handedly. "But I really am sorry about all this. I shouldn't have been so forceful in making you buy me out."

"That's all right. I probably would've done the same thing if I'd been in your shoes." The fact that he was trying to make her feel better made her feel even worse. But she guessed that was just the kind of person he was. She'd just been too blind to see it all these years. "Hell. I'm sorry, Sam, but isn't this Carla's charity? Forget what I said. I don't want to make you feel uncomfortable."

"Don't worry about it," she assured him. "I was going to go anyway, and I would rather go with you if I had the choice." No matter how much she told herself that it didn't matter that one of the women Jason had been seeing would be at the gala, it did, and it would be nice to not have to go alone.

"Thanks, Samantha. I really appreciate it."

"Do you want me to issue some kind of a statement?"

"No. I figure going to the gala together should be enough to settle any rumors. A statement would just be overkill."

He was probably right. One of the things she looked at as an analyst was how a company's management handled certain situations. If it seemed as if they were overcompensating for something, it was usually because they were.

"Is everything all right?" Cindy asked when she hung up a minute later.

Sam sighed as she put her phone away. "Luke is facing some backlash over me selling Jason's half of the company to him."

"That sucks."

"Yeah. He's hoping the press seeing us together at a gala will help clear the air."

Cindy laughed. "How will you sniping at him in public be good for him?"

"I don't snipe."

Her sister shrugged. "Generally you don't, but Luke is another matter. I've only met him a few times, and most of those times, you've had something bad to say about him if not to him."

Sam winced at the reminder of how badly she'd treated Luke over the years. She'd thought he was the bad guy when, in fact, he was the best of the best.

"I made a mistake," she admitted. "He's a good guy."

"I doubt it, but I get it. You've never been the kind of person to say something bad about someone until this Luke guy. It was only time until you returned to your normal self. I'm just surprised it lasted this long. Now, finish your croissant. I don't want to be late to the show."

Sam quickly ate her croissant and finished her drink, but as they left the coffee shop, guilt crept into her. It seemed as if she couldn't do anything right where Luke was concerned. First, with calling him a liar. Then, with sleeping with him. And if that weren't enough, she'd practically forced him to buy her out.

She sure hoped going to the gala with him would clear the rumors. She hated to think of all the troubles she'd given to him while she'd gotten away from everything scot-free. She glanced at her sister and sighed when she saw the excitement in Cindy's eyes as she took in the theater's marquee. At least, she'd gotten something right.

CHAPTER THIRTEEN

He shouldn't have invited Sam to the gala.

Luke inwardly cursed as he got out of the elevator in Sam's apartment building. He should've just allowed her to issue some kind of a statement. Instead, he'd leapt at the chance to spend time with her. It didn't seem to matter that she wasn't interested in him in the romantic sense and that he was only fooling himself—hoping for things that wouldn't be. The plain truth was that he'd missed her.

And that desire to see her again was making him do crazy things. When he normally went to a gala, he usually just grabbed the first tux he saw in his closet. But with Sam, he actually cared about how he looked. Maybe it was because she was used to going with Jason, who'd always dressed to the nines, but Luke had wanted to look good for her and had gotten a new tux and shoes even though he had plenty of perfectly good ones at home.

He shook his head at his own foolishness and rapped on her apartment door. This was the last time he did something like this again. It was too much effort and for what? To impress someone who'd already told him that she didn't want to be with him?

Insane. He was definitely insane.

The door opened a moment later and his throat dried at the sight. She was wearing a beautiful white gown that ran from her shoulders to her toes, skimming her curves in all the right places. He ached to have her in his arms once again and he was suddenly grateful for putting the extra effort into dressing up tonight. Hell, he'd go through that stupid tux fitting a hundred times just to hold her for five minutes. Remembering just how well her body molded to his, he groaned. He wasn't sure how he was going to make it through the night without trying something he shouldn't.

Sam's breath hitched at the heat in Luke's eyes as he took in her gown. He was looking at her as if she were a dessert—one he'd very much like to devour. Though she'd been hoping that he'd like the dress, she'd never thought that this would be the reaction she'd get and was suddenly grateful that she'd chosen to go with the unknown designer. Luke blinked, and the heat in his eyes disappeared and was replaced by a cool, impassive gaze.

"You ready?" he asked.

She sighed. What had she been hoping for? That he'd take one look at her, take her into his arms, and kiss her the way he'd done two months ago? That he wouldn't be able to resist her and drag her to the nearest bedroom? She would've laughed if she wasn't being so ridiculous. The only reason he was with her tonight was to quell a business rumor—not date her and she would do well to remember that.

"Yeah," she murmured, trying not to let the hurt dig into her. She didn't know why she was disappointed. It wasn't as if she were ready for a relationship anyway. Getting a new gown to impress him had been a crazy idea when she already had enough gowns for a lifetime.

"Let me just get my clutch." She let go of the door and went to get her bag. "So…do you have a game plan for tonight?" she asked as she walked back towards him and tried not to think about how well he filled his tux. She was a sucker for a man in a tux and Luke filled his out nicely. The jacket hugged his broad shoulders and she couldn't help but remember how strong those muscles had felt when she'd run her hands all over him.

Dark eyebrows rose. "Game plan?"

Her cheeks burning as though he could read her thoughts, she forced herself to look away from those shoulders and meet his eyes. "You know, people you want to talk with." She shrugged. "People you want to avoid…"

"Not really, although Hank did tell me to make myself more accessible."

She could just imagine how that talk must have gone. Before Jason's death, Luke had always done his best to avoid meeting their clients. He hadn't wanted to take time away from important work for what he regarded as hand-holding.

"Not that it really matters," he continued as they made

their way towards the door. "People always seem to find me at these things anyways. How about you? Any CEOs or CFOs you want to corner?"

Touched that he remembered that she'd started investing on her own, she smiled. "No. This is strictly personal for me. Jason's parents expect me to be there."

But this year would be the last time she did anything like this. Just because she wouldn't tell them about Jason's affairs didn't mean she intended to play the grieving widow forever. She needed time away from all of this to find herself again.

"Have you talked with them recently?" Luke asked as she locked the door to her apartment.

"Jessica calls about once a week." Which was a lot better than when she used to visit every day. Sam loved her mother-in-law, but she had no desire to hear any more stories about the woman's beloved son.

Luke sighed. "I know I should visit them, but I've been busy."

Sam waved him off. "I'm sure they understand. Besides, you'll see them tonight. I'm sure they'll want to thank you when they hear about the new hospital wing that'll be named after Jason."

"I was just continuing Jason's donations," he said and Sam's lips quirked.

She knew he'd donated a lot more than what Jason usually had or they wouldn't be naming a hospital wing after Jason. But as always, Luke was being modest.

"Let me know if tonight becomes too much. I can

pretend that I have to leave for work and that you offered to help."

She laughed. "I vaguely remember you using work as an excuse to leave early last year, and possibly the year before." He'd often disappear as soon as they'd finished their hellos.

Luke shrugged. "Hey, it works. Just let me know if you want to get out, okay?"

The fact that Luke was prepared to let her call the shots eased some of her anxiety about whom she might run into tonight. It was reassuring to know that she could leave at any time.

"All right. Thank you."

* * *

Sam froze as they walked into the glitzy ballroom and she saw all the beautiful women there. *Exactly how many of them had slept with Jason?*

She suddenly felt sick as she remembered all the names and pictures she'd seen on his phone. She wasn't ready for this. She was about to take a step back when Luke tightened his arm around her and murmured, "Do you want to get something to drink?"

His hot breath tickled her skin, sending shivers down her spine, and she was grateful for the opportunity to focus on something other than her tempestuous thoughts.

"Sure." One night. All she had to do was survive tonight and she wouldn't force herself to do anything like this ever again.

Without loosening his hold, Luke guided her towards the bar at the back of the room. Though she knew that it was just a PR stunt, she smiled at the realization that he wasn't going to leave her the way Jason always had at these things. Jason had often said that he was going to get them drinks before he'd get drawn into a conversation and forget all about her until it was time for dinner.

Some people stopped to greet her and Luke. There were a few pitying looks, but not as many as she'd expected. The majority of them wanted to grill Luke about Harkin or to ask how he felt about a certain industry or company. It didn't take long before she realized that his grip around her tightened whenever someone new approached. It was as if he were drawing strength from her or perhaps he was trying to remember his reason for being there in case he felt the urge to snap at them.

She could just imagine how thin his patience must be running. She'd seen him in more client meetings during her last few weeks at Harkin than she'd had in all the years she'd worked at the company. And as if that weren't enough, he now had to attend these functions and make small talk as well?

It was so different than what she was used to seeing of him, and she couldn't help but admire him for everything that he was doing to save Harkin. While other hedge fund managers would've just downsized their companies without a thought to the people who'd lose their jobs, Luke was probably already operating at a loss. She doubted that the management fees they'd make this year would cover their payroll and yet, he hadn't laid a single person off.

She knew that he was trying to get back the business that they'd lost, and hoped he was successful. There was no one she knew who was more deserving.

They had just gotten their drinks when a woman in a revealing black dress bumped into Luke. The blonde's hands rose to his chest and Sam didn't miss the napkin the woman put in the pocket of his tuxedo as she patted him.

"Excuse me," she murmured as she looked at Luke with bedroom eyes and trailed her hands down his tux. The woman glanced at Sam then, as if she didn't see her as a threat, looked back at Luke, and mouthed, "Call me," before walking away, her hips swaying seductively.

Jealousy stabbed Sam. Even if Luke didn't call this woman, she knew that there were plenty of other gorgeous women who were interested in him—many of them in this room. She hadn't missed the glances they'd thrown his way tonight.

They hadn't even bothered hiding their interest, and she couldn't help but think that this was like being with Jason all over again. Except this time, she was consciously aware of what was happening instead of deluding herself that her husband was being faithful to her.

"Sorry," Luke said.

Sam waved him off. "It's nothing."

Thank goodness she hadn't agreed to continue seeing him or this jealousy would've been a lot worse. No matter what she'd been feeling for Luke since they'd slept together, it wasn't as if she had a claim on him.

He'd given her a chance to explore a relationship between them and she'd refused. So, she shouldn't be jealous if he decided to meet up with the woman who'd bumped into him later tonight. She inwardly groaned at her own foolishness. What was she even thinking? She'd seen the woman. It wasn't a question of if he would call her, it was when.

"Do you want to see what's up for auction?" Luke asked.

"You don't have to babysit me." She was sure he had better things to do than to stay with her throughout the night, but she appreciated the effort. He probably wanted to protect her from Carla, but she didn't want to be a pity case—especially not to him. "I'm sure the press got enough pictures of us outside," she continued. No one would think they were at odds now.

"Reneging already?"

"Reneging on what, exactly?"

"On being my date."

She laughed at the unexpectedness of the question. He was making it seem as if it was a privilege to be with her when, in reality, it was the other way around. It struck her then what she'd given up when she'd slept with him. She could've really used a friend like him. He was kind and thoughtful and yet, he didn't pull any punches. He always told things as they were, even if you didn't want to hear it.

Too bad he made her think of sex whenever she looked at him.

"All right," she said, nodding. "Have it your way. Let's go look at the auction pieces."

Hopefully, Madeline was able to get José Patron to donate the private cooking lesson she'd been working on getting. It would be a wonderful birthday present for Cindy. Her sister loved his show.

Determined to stop obsessing about Luke and whether or not he was going to take the woman home tonight, Sam vowed to win the cooking lesson.

* * *

"Samantha."

Sam tensed at the familiar voice. It was Tom Williams—Carla's husband. Knowing that she couldn't ignore the man, she excused herself from Jason's parents. As soon as she turned around, she was engulfed in a big hug. His strong cologne made her feel like sneezing and she quickly stepped away before she did just that.

"Hi, Tom."

"It's good to see you, Sam," he said as he smiled at her. "Carla and I were worried that you weren't going to come this year."

Sam inwardly groaned. With all her worries about coming tonight, she hadn't even thought about whether or not she should tell Tom about Carla. Considering how nice he was being to her, she doubted he knew about the affair. But at the same time, she didn't want to make things hard on Carla, either. Though she'd just been one of the many women Jason had been seeing, Carla might truly have felt something for Jason. If Tom didn't know about the affair already, Sam might just be giving Carla more trouble on top of the heartbreak she was already enduring.

But what if she were a serial cheater like Jason? Or what if Tom and Carla had an open marriage?

She didn't know why she was giving Carla any consideration when Carla had obviously never spared the same for her and suddenly wished that she'd just stayed at home instead of trying to prove to herself that she wasn't going to hide. She didn't even like attending these things, but she hadn't wanted Jason's infidelity to take more from her than it already had.

"I already feel bad about not being able to take up Jason's duties," she said, and suddenly felt a huge amount of respect for Luke for having the guts to tell her that Jason had been cheating on her. She and Luke hadn't even really been friends when he'd told her and yet he had, risking his best friend's ire for her.

If only she'd listened to him.

"Oh. Don't you worry about that," Tom said. "After so many years of putting on this event, we're a well-oiled machine."

Sympathy shone in Tom's eyes and Sam knew that he was about to talk about Jason. Hoping to change topics before he could even mention Jason, she asked Tom about his all-time favorite topic—his children.

He was going to hell.

Luke groaned as he forced himself to look away from Samantha's deliciously shaped ass as she spoke with one of the directors of the charity. It was bad enough that he'd practically drooled over her when he'd picked her up earlier, but he just couldn't stop looking at her. Those beautiful almond-shaped eyes, those curves... He wanted nothing more than to grab hold of her ass and slide deep inside of her. *Fuck.* He wasn't just going to hell. He was sure they had a special place reserved just for him.

"I'd love to come by to talk more about our project."

Luke blinked and focused on the young redhead in front of him. Guilt bit into him at the realization that he hadn't listened to a single word she'd said since she'd approached him. All he knew was that she was part of some charity that was undoubtedly looking for a donation.

"I'm pretty swamped with work right now," he admitted. "Can you send over your prospectus to my assistant?" Sheila knew what kind of charities he was interested in and was adept at sifting through these things.

"I—Of course. Thank you for your time."

She stood and left, and almost immediately, Adam Campbell took the vacated seat. "I can't believe I caught you. Don't you always have some kind of business 'emergency' you have to get to?"

Luke grinned at his friend. He hadn't seen him in ages. They'd met through Jason and frankly, Adam was the only one of Jason's friends Luke truly liked. Though he'd been born into one of the country's richest families, Adam hadn't used that as an excuse to slack off. He worked hard and over the years had developed a small empire of properties around the South. Luke wouldn't be surprised if his company's profits would one day surpass those of the cosmetics company his great-grandfather had founded.

Along with Jason, the three of them would often go out for drinks or dinner, but Luke had just been so swamped these past few months that those get-togethers hadn't happened. Between Jason's death, the Cervco trade, Peter quitting, and Sam leaving, it seemed as if Luke were battling fight after fight.

"Not this year." Luke nodded towards Sam. "I brought Sam along with me."

He doubted she'd mind leaving early, but he didn't want to be the reason she missed out on that auction item she wanted for her sister. Besides, for the first time, he didn't want to leave a gala early. Since he didn't know when he would see her next, he would make this night last as long as he could.

"You came with someone?" Adam's eyebrows rose with interest before he turned and spotted Sam. "Oh, man. That's nice of you. How's she doing?"

"As well as you can expect," Luke answered and frowned. Did people think he'd taken her to the gala as some kind of charity case?

"It's good to see her out and about. She and Jason were so close." Adam shook his head and gestured to him. "And it's good thinking on your part. You've got a beautiful, fun date who won't get any ideas of things being permanent. Hell, I should've asked her to come with me."

Luke's fist clenched at the thought of Adam holding Sam the way Luke had tonight. He didn't want her to be in anyone's arms except *his*. He knew that his feelings were a bit territorial for someone who'd already been rejected by her, but he just couldn't stop himself. In his head, she belonged with *him*.

"I don't think she really likes going to these things," he said, though he didn't know for sure. All he knew was that he didn't want Adam asking her out. "She just came, because of the tribute," he continued, not even feeling an ounce of guilt for using Jason as an excuse to ward Adam off.

"Oh. Right. I forgot about that." Adam sighed. "I guess I just have to find another woman to bring along to these things."

As if he would have any problem getting a date. With his wealth and looks, Adam didn't even have to crook a finger to get a date. Hoping to change topics, Luke asked, "So how's your project in Texas going?"

Though Sam had rejected him, he wasn't quite sure that she'd reject Adam. Like Jason, Adam was charming and handsome, and Luke wasn't about to take that risk. He'd already had to put up with seeing her with Jason all these years. Seeing her with Adam might just about kill him.

"Great. We finally got the zoning approved." As Adam started talking about the apartment complex he was building, Luke inwardly shook his head. He couldn't believe that he'd gotten jealous over the thought of Adam asking Sam out when he knew that Adam wasn't looking for anything more than an innocent date.

Though seeing her tonight had been a balm to his soul, Luke knew that he couldn't afford to do so again. She was wreaking havoc all over him to the point that he couldn't think properly. What's worse was that the more time he spent with her, the greater the chance that he'd do something foolish like grabbing her and kissing her the way he'd thought of doing a hundred times tonight. And since he was having such a hard time controlling himself around her, he was going to have to go cold turkey no matter how much it hurt.

CHAPTER FOURTEEN

"Thanks for taking me to the gala," Sam said as she they walked into her apartment later that night. "I had fun."

But her words fell on deaf ears. All Luke could think about was how beautiful she looked in that dress and how he'd wanted to punch all the men he'd caught looking at her tonight. He wished he had the right to call her his, but she didn't want him that way. She'd made herself more than clear all those weeks ago.

But even the knowledge that she didn't want him couldn't stop him from wanting her with every fiber of his being. Not knowing when he would see her again, he felt desperation bite at him. How long would it be until he saw her next? Months? Years?

The uncertainty of it all drove him to do what he'd been thinking about doing all night. He kissed her. She gasped at the contact, and he took advantage, deepening the kiss as he wrapped his arms around her. He didn't dare loosen his grip and risk her moving away. If this was the last kiss he would have from her, he would make it last as long as he could.

As if he could get her to return his feelings, he put everything he had into the kiss—all the frustration he'd felt these past few weeks without her, how much he'd missed her, all the words he couldn't say…

Triumph coursed through him when she softened in his arms and kissed him back. He groaned. He'd missed this. So damn much. The taste of her, the feel of her… But the sensations reminded him of just how hard things have been these past few weeks, how he'd known exactly what he was missing every second he was away from her. It had been one thing to fantasize about her for all these years, but now that he knew the taste of her and the sweet sound of her moan when he nibbled her neck, not being with her was torture. Absolute torture. He couldn't do it again. He couldn't have heaven for one night just to have it snatched away in the morning again.

Calling himself a hundred times a fool, he broke their kiss and bent his forehead to hers. Already, he missed the taste of her lips.

"I'm sorry, Sam," he said as he stepped away. "I can't do this. I don't think I can handle you turning me away again." He shouldn't have even started anything, but he hadn't been able to stop himself. He'd wanted her for so long that it had become his second nature.

"What if I don't turn you away?" she murmured after a few seconds as her hands began to roam his chest, sending licks of pleasure coursing through him.

"What do you mean?" Though his head was telling himself not to jump to conclusions, he felt hope spread through him like rapid fire.

She shrugged as her hands continued roaming his chest. "A fling for however long this attraction lasts between us."

Which meant however long she was willing to see him. Because he couldn't imagine a scenario where he wouldn't want to be with her.

Though he didn't like the thought of never knowing when she would end things, he knew that a fling was the best he could ask for right now. He'd wanted her for years, but everything was still new to her. Hell, she'd been in love with another man up until a few weeks ago.

"A secret fling," she continued as she looked up at him with those dark eyes of hers. "Though I know what we're doing isn't wrong, I don't want people thinking differently of me, either."

He couldn't care less what other people thought about them, but since it was important to her, he nodded. He'd have her anyway he could.

"So, you agree?" she asked, a smile appearing on her lips—lips that he could kiss anytime he wanted if he agreed to the fling.

His head felt dizzy at the thought. He knew he should say no. Sam wasn't a fling type of a girl, and there was a big chance that he was just setting himself up for a bigger heartbreak. But he'd forever regret it if he said no. Sure, she was agreeing to a fling now, but what if he could get her to fall for him along the way? He'd never know unless he tried.

He nodded as he cupped her face. "I do," he said before he kissed her, sealing the deal. Her tongue met his as her arms went around him. Groaning, he ran his hands over her curves, memorizing every inch of her with his hands as he made a trail of kisses down her neck. She moaned, and the sound went straight to his cock.

He lifted her into his arms. "Bedroom?"

She pointed behind her and he quickly moved. He turned on the lights before setting her down next to the bed, making a line of hot kisses down her throat as he did so. He unzipped the dress that he'd admired all night and felt his throat go dry when he saw the lace bra cupping her supple breasts and her sheer black panties. No matter how many times he'd thought about her, it just wasn't the same as seeing her in the flesh.

She took advantage of his momentary lapse and reached for his tux. Eager to undress her as well, he reached for the hooks of her bra. The fabric fell away and the sight of her bare breasts made his head light. He cupped one and brushed a thumb softly over her nipple. Her eyes fluttered, and he brought the hardened point to his mouth. She gasped as he laved her, her hand running through his hair and pulling. Smiling, he continued licking and sucking her before moving to the other breast, loving the way her back arched and her breath hitched.

His hand roamed her belly before he moved lower, peppering kisses down her stomach then down to her panties. She gasped as he kissed her through the fabric. He flashed her a grin before he rolled her panties off and groaned when he found her wet.

He quickly removed his shirt and pants and went back to her open arms. He kissed her, loving the way she ran her hands greedily over his back as if she couldn't get enough of him. Right then, he knew that he loved her. There was no other way to explain how he felt and why she was always on his mind. Immediately wanting to tell her, he pulled away.

"Samantha, I—"

"I'm on the pill," she interrupted him, and he cursed himself. They'd agreed to a no strings attached fling—not love. No matter how he felt about her, he had to remind himself that she didn't want him that way. At least, not yet.

Thank goodness she'd stopped him before his declaration scared her off or made her think that he took the words lightly. He'd never forgive himself if he messed this up.

"I'm clean," he said instead, awed that she would trust him. He'd never gone without a condom before. He'd never trusted a woman enough to risk it. But deep down, he doubted he'd mind if something happened. The thought of being connected to Sam forever was a heady one. He'd never worry about whether or not he would see her again, because they'd be a family. His chest tightened at the thought of a little girl that looked like Sam or a little boy with her eyes. He wanted everything with Sam, he realized. The house, the family…everything.

She nodded. "Me, too."

Loving that she trusted him, he groaned as he kissed her. As their tongues tangled, he entered her. Delicious sensations coursed through him at the feel of her around him. Damn. How he'd missed this. How he'd missed *her*. In awe, he began moving.

Her hands gripped his butt, urging him on. He didn't have to be told twice. He hooked one of her legs behind him and moved faster. Moaning, she wrapped her other leg around him, pushing him deeper inside of her. He groaned at the sensation. He wouldn't last long. It had been too long and he wanted her too much.

But he wanted to make this as good for her as it was for him, so he began running the earnings per share of a shale company he'd been looking at earlier, hoping he could last a little longer. But when her inner walls began to spasm around him, he couldn't control himself any longer. Knowing it wouldn't be long, he reached for her clit. She moaned as she trembled beneath him, and it was the sexiest sound he'd ever heard. He dug himself into her, groaning as he came. Depleted, he burrowed his face into her hair, inhaling the sweet scent of vanilla. He'd never come so hard in his life. He was completely and utterly spent. Smiling, he collapsed beside her.

"That. Was. Amazing," Sam said a minute later as she turned towards him.

Male pride burst through him as he looked at her. She looked like a woman well-loved. Her cheeks were flushed, and her lips swollen. And the fact that it had been him who'd put that look on her face? Unbelievable.

"Well. I'm glad you thought so, because I'm pretty sure you just about killed me."

She laughed, and the sound was like a sweet balm to his

ears. He gathered her into his arms and felt his chest tighten at how right this all felt. He'd give anything to have her in his arms like this every night. He didn't know how, but somehow, he was going to make it happen.

CHAPTER FIFTEEN

Luke watched Sam sleep longer than he should have Monday morning. Wary of anyone finding out how he felt about her, he'd always been mindful about getting caught looking at her. But now that he could look at her anytime he pleased, he was finding it hard to stop. She was just so damn beautiful.

But he really should get going.

There were probably people already looking for him at the office, and he still had all that work that he was supposed to have done over the weekend but hadn't. Sighing, he brushed a kiss over Sam's forehead and gently removed his arm from under her. His feet felt like lead as he stood. He didn't want to leave. He wanted to wake her up with a kiss then make love some more, but he had responsibilities and a company to run.

"Luke?"

He turned and saw that he'd woken her up, though barely. Her eyes drooping, she looked like she would fall asleep at any moment. Knowing that he wouldn't get to again until tonight, he leaned over and kissed her. Her soft lips gave way to his tongue and her sweet taste exploded in his mouth. He bit her bottom lip and felt himself harden at the sound of her moan. Groaning, he straightened. If he didn't leave right now, he wouldn't leave at all.

"I have to go to work," he said, already missing her. He'd never spent the night with a woman before. He'd never felt the desire to. But with Sam, he was quickly finding that he wanted to spend all his time with her. One night had easily become three and he could see it becoming a lot more just as easily. It was insane. This weekend should've helped alleviate this hunger he felt for her, but if anything, it had made it worse.

"Oh." Her eyes widened when she looked at the clock on the nightstand. "Of course," she said as she straightened and his blood hummed. If she sat up any straighter, the bed sheet would reveal those supple breasts and he'd be even later. "Wow. You're usually there by now," she said as she tucked her hair behind her ear.

"Yeah, but I don't usually have a nympho surprising me in the middle of the night." Her cheeks flushed a deep red, and he grinned. He didn't know how she could look so cute and sexy at the same time. "Have lunch with me today," he said impulsively. He didn't want to spend a whole day without seeing her.

She frowned. "You want to take me out to lunch?"

He nodded, and she shook her head. "I'm sorry, Luke, but I already made plans with my sister. Besides, I thought we agreed to keep this thing under wraps."

His stomach dropped at the reminder that what they had was just a fling—that what they had was just temporary. At some point over the weekend, he'd tricked himself into thinking that what they had was more than sex—that what they had was real.

"I know. I wasn't thinking." All he could think about was seeing her again. But perhaps it was a good thing she'd said no. It wasn't like he had the time to take her out. This weekend had already put him behind at work. Going out to lunch would just make him even more behind. "Have fun with Cindy today. I guess I'll see you later, then?" Relief coursed through him when she nodded. At least, she wasn't having second thoughts. "I can have Maria make pot roast."

"I love pot roast, but Maria—"

"She's usually gone by three," he said, hoping to ease her worries. He found his shirt on the floor and picked it up. "And I'll give her tomorrow morning off." And any other morning he needed in order to keep Sam in his bed. Heat rushed over him at the memory of Sam's dark hair spread out over his pillow, her soft lips parted as he moved in and out of her. His blood rushed south, and he quickly began thinking of all the things he would do when he went to the office. When he had better control of himself, he continued, "I figure we can figure out breakfast by ourselves."

"I can make eggs," Sam said, smiling.

Knowing how much she hated to cook, he felt his heart soften. She might not love him, but she was willing to do something she didn't like just to be with him.

"I like the way you think," he murmured. He put on his

shirt then grabbed his pants. He looked back at Sam and resisted the urge to go to her. He still had to go to his place and change. He quickly put on his pants. "I'll see you tonight."

* * *

Luke dropped the report he was reading and rubbed his eyes. He'd just spent the last twenty minutes on the same sentence with no luck. Tidbits of the past weekend kept flitting in and out of his mind, distracting him to no end—of how cozy it had been to eat breakfast with Sam in her apartment yesterday, of how sexy she looked when she came, of how warm and inviting she'd looked when he'd left her this morning… He shook his head and picked up the report again. The faster he stopped daydreaming, the sooner he could get home.

The image of a naked Sam greeting him in bed flashed through his head and he grinned. He could definitely get used to this. He was just thinking of all the different things they could do together when his intercom buzzed and Sheila's voice filled the air. "Mark Lang's office just called. They can meet you for dinner at seven."

Luke ran a hand down his face and bit back a curse. He'd been trying to get a call with the Jellmeck CEO for the past two months to talk about their expansion plans without any luck. Today was the first time the man had agreed to talk with him, and he doubted the man would give him another chance if he declined today's invitation.

"Go ahead and confirm the dinner," he told his assistant.

He hated canceling on Sam, but he had to do this. Jellmeck was quickly becoming one of the fund's biggest holdings, but he had some concerns about their expansion plans into the Midwest. There was a competing Wisconsin chain of paint shops that was also branching out into Illinois and he had serious doubts about the both of them surviving there.

"Sure thing, boss."

His shoulders slumped as Sheila disconnected. He'd really been looking forward to seeing Sam, but business came first. As he got his phone out, he wondered whether or not he could still go to Sam's apartment after the meeting.

He could probably get there by eleven. *But what if the meeting ran late?* The dinner could very well end at one. He couldn't ask Sam to wait up for him. His stomach dropped at the realization that he wouldn't be seeing her tonight. Sighing, he picked up his phone. Tomorrow, he vowed to himself. Tomorrow, he would see her.

* * *

She was way over her head.

Samantha tightened her grip around the basket of muffins she'd had her cook bake. She'd told herself that this was going to be a fling and yet, she was practically bouncing at the thought of seeing Luke again. She'd missed him far more than she should've after he'd called to cancel yesterday, and she'd found herself counting the hours until she would see him again today. That wasn't normal, was it? She couldn't remember ever feeling or acting this way with Jason or Ben, her boyfriend before Jason.

Butterflies flew in her stomach as she watched the numbers on the elevator screen quickly zoom by. She'd been surprised to learn that Luke hadn't revoked her security access to his private elevator since he'd had it registered all those years ago, but she was grateful. It saved her a lot of embarrassment from having to see the doorman whenever she came over.

She stepped out of the elevator and into Luke's living room. From across the room, Luke's gaze met hers, and her heart skipped a beat. With his sleeves rolled up and the top buttons of his shirt undone, he looked devilishly handsome.

Heat rose in her cheeks as his gaze roamed appreciatively over her before it slowly rose up. It was as if he'd touched her with his eyes. Straightening, he put down the report he'd been reading and walked towards her. They met halfway, and within seconds, he was kissing her in a way that had her wishing she could melt into him. She could kiss him all day.

He pulled away a minute later and smiled. "I've been waiting to do that all day," he murmured as he cupped her face and brushed his thumb over her lips. Instantly, her nerves were gone. Thank goodness she wasn't the only one feeling this way.

She smiled as she set the basket down. "How was work?"

He groaned as he leaned his forehead onto hers. "I spent all day thinking about you and when I finally see you, you want to talk about work? I'm definitely doing something wrong."

Without warning, he picked her up. Laughing, she wrapped her arms around him and kissed him as they headed towards the bedroom.

CHAPTER SIXTEEN

"I can't believe you're making me watch a chick flick," Luke said as they both settled into the couch in his apartment a month later.

"Stop complaining," Sam said as she lightly smacked his shoulder. "You know you love it." Who wouldn't love a movie about two best friends falling in love with a lot of wacky characters and escapades to boot?

He wrapped his arm around her, and her insides melted. She liked being in his arms and loved the fact that his couch allowed for it. His setup was so unlike Jason's private theater, which had had humongous reclining seats and large divides between the chairs for the control panels and cup holders. It'd been hard enough to hold hands, let alone snuggle.

With Luke's couch, she could lean on his shoulder or lie down with her head on his lap. And it wasn't just the couch she liked. She felt more at home at Luke's apartment than she'd ever felt in that big house, though she knew that might have more to do with the man himself. There was just something about Luke that felt right.

"Or maybe I just like the sex during it," Luke said, his eyes darkening as he tilted his head towards her.

Her cheeks burned as she remembered how she'd ridden him on this very couch the last time they'd tried to watch a movie. At first, he'd only been making soft circles around her shoulder and her wrist, but those soft touches had wreaked havoc over her entire body. Before she'd known it, he'd had her on his lap and was kissing and petting her to dizzying pleasure.

And then when he'd guided her down on his hardness... She shivered at the memory of how full he'd felt inside of her.

Mischief shone in his eyes as he smiled, and she suspected that he was remembering the same thing. How was he still having this effect on her? They'd been seeing each other for a month now, and if anything, it seemed as if she was becoming even *more* addicted to him.

She knew she was acting as if she were a teenager who'd just discovered sex, but Luke made her feel things she'd never felt before. Maybe it was because they'd known each other before they'd slept together. Or maybe it was because he was one of the few people who knew some of the secrets of her marriage and supported her regardless. Whatever the reason, it was just so easy being with him. He accepted her as she was without asking for more.

Knowing that she would lose all train of thought the moment he put his hands on her, she pulled away. "Oh, no. We're going to finish this movie this time." Though she'd already watched it a hundred times, she'd never seen it with him.

"Sure we are," he said as he dragged her onto his lap and captured her lips in a kiss. Heat curled inside of her as their tongues mated. His hands dipped under her shirt and spanned her stomach. By the time he'd cupped a breast, she'd forgotten all about the movie.

As they lay in bed an hour later, Luke sunk his nose into Samantha's hair, breathed in the vanilla scent, and sighed in satisfaction. Life didn't get any better than this. Because he couldn't stop himself, he began a line of kisses over her neck and shoulder. Moaning, she tilted her head, giving him better access and he smiled. He loved how in sync their minds were.

He had just moved to the top of her spine when the phone rang. Not wanting to stop, he continued making his way down her back. Hopefully, the person calling would get the message and call again tomorrow. After a few more rings, Sam turned around to face him. "Don't you want to get that?"

Knowing that it could be important, he ran a hand through his hair and sighed. "Yeah. Of course."

He pulled away from her and immediately felt a sense of loss as he stood. The next time she came over to his place, he was going to disconnect the phone and turn off his cell. He didn't want anyone interrupting their time together.

"Yeah?" he answered as he picked up the call. He

looked at the bed to find Sam watching him and already regretted getting up. *Why did she have to be so damn responsible?* He just wanted to spend all night in bed with Sam—to hell with work.

"Pillar wants to borrow ten million," George said. "They need a deal by tonight or they're going to go to McFadden."

Reality interrupted into his thoughts and Luke groaned. Work was work. If they stopped entertaining deals just because of the time, no one would think to call them when they needed a quick cash infusion.

"Call the team to meet at the office in an hour," he told his manager.

He grimaced as he ended the call and turned to Sam. "I have to go to the office."

"That's all right," she said as she straightened. His eyes immediately went to her pert breasts and his throat dried. "Anything I can help with?"

Her question shook him out of his thoughts, and disappointment roiled through him at how understanding she always was when something like this happened before he cursed himself. Why was he disappointed that she was being so understanding? He didn't actually want her to whine and ask him to come back to bed, did he?

Okay. Maybe he did. He wanted her to fight him a little, so that he would, at least, know that this need he felt for her wasn't just one-sided. Knowing that that wasn't going to happen anytime soon, he forced the thought from his head and smiled. "No, but thanks. I appreciate the offer."

As he left the apartment, he reminded himself that it

should be enough he had her in his life. And with that last reminder, he put his mind to what awaited him at the office.

* * *

Luke watched unseeingly as the analysts argued over the terms of their offer two hours later. He still couldn't get over the fact that Sam never complained about his hours or even looked disappointed whenever he had to leave early. In fact, she'd been so understanding she'd offered to help!

Though he knew that her marriage with Jason had accustomed her to cancelled dates and late birthday celebrations, he didn't want it to be like that between them. She deserved so much more. He'd told himself that he would never take her for granted the way Jason had, and here he was doing exactly that.

Luke suddenly noticed how quiet the room had become and saw everyone looking at him expectedly.

"I'm sorry, what?"

Clark leaned forward. "How many board seats do you want to take?"

Trying to remember the conversation before his thoughts had wandered to Sam, he racked his brain and answered, "Three. Though their business model is solid, their recent sales leave a lot for wanting. We need to keep an eye on things—especially on how their new chip compares to their competitors."

Any of which he couldn't name at this particular moment. Hell, considering where his head was at, he shouldn't have even bothered to come tonight. Even now,

191

all he could think about was how he shouldn't have answered the phone and how he wished that she'd stayed at his apartment. Some caveman part of him liked the thought of Sam sleeping in his bed even if he wasn't there with her. But it wouldn't have been fair to ask her to stay when he hadn't even known if he could get back tonight.

"I told you," he heard Mike say as he slapped his palm on the table. "They'd be suicidal not to take the deal."

Luke inwardly sighed as he thought about how he'd still be in bed with Sam if he hadn't come to the office. They didn't really need him here, did they? These guys had their system down pat. He was more of a referee than anything. George or one of the other managers would undoubtedly be able to handle it. He'd just never given them the chance.

He would in the future, he suddenly decided. Maybe these late-night meetings were one of the things he had to step away from now that he'd taken over some of Jason's responsibilities. Sure, he'd come in if they requested it of him, but he wouldn't automatically. Besides, he always checked the larger deals before approving them anyway.

Some of the burden he'd been carrying since Jason's death lifted with the decision. He trusted his employees, so why hadn't he been willing to hand off the work to them? The idea niggled at him, and he attributed it to his usual inability to delegate. It would be an adjustment for him to share responsibility with someone other than Jason, but if he wanted to spend more time with Sam, something had to give. And he did want to spend his time with her.

CHAPTER SEVENTEEN

"There's something different about you," Adam said as he put his drink down a week later and considered Luke.

Feeling guilty that he hadn't made an effort to see his friend since he'd started seeing Sam, Luke had finally agreed to meet him for lunch. He usually ate lunch in the office, but he hadn't wanted to cut his time with Sam short. He already only got to see her during nights and weekends. He wasn't about to waste one of those nights with Adam, regardless of how much his friend meant to him.

"I got it," Adam said as he snapped his fingers. "You're smiling. It's a girl, isn't it?"

Luke frowned. He'd thought some of the people in the office had been looking at him strangely lately. Was it because he was smiling? He hadn't realized he'd been doing it, but it was probably true. He couldn't remember ever being this happy. He couldn't get enough of Sam and thankfully, it seemed as if she couldn't get enough of him, either.

He suddenly wished he could tell Adam about Sam. Not only did he not like hiding something so important from one of his closest friends, but he was just so happy he wanted to tell everyone the news. But since Sam didn't want anyone knowing about them, he shrugged as he picked up his glass.

"I could have a business deal in the works," he said before taking a drink.

His friend laughed. "Now I know it's not a business deal, because I just spoke with Hank the other day and all he did was complain about redemptions."

Luke froze in surprise. He hadn't known Adam and Hank were friends.

"So a woman, eh? Is that why you've been so busy lately?"

"I'm sorry I've been AWOL so much," Luke lied. He'd much rather spend the night with Sam than with one of the guys, but doubted his friend would appreciate him saying so.

"Yeah. I'm sure you are. So when will I meet this woman who's got your panties all twisted in a bunch?"

Luke frowned when he suddenly realized how bad things would look when he and Sam came out with their relationship. He doubted even Adam, who knew about Jason's affairs, would be accepting. He'd think Luke was violating a bro code or worse, was taking advantage of Sam at a time she was feeling vulnerable. And maybe Luke was.

Though he'd told himself he'd been helping her forget about Jason when she'd come to him that first night, he also knew that he would have made up any excuse to be with her. And it wasn't as if he could stop seeing her. He already felt uneasy when he didn't see her for a day. He wasn't sure how he was going to handle it if she ever broke up with him.

But the fact that it had taken him this long to realize how bad things could look if people found out about them was a testament to how Sam affected him. All he could think about when he was with her was her.

"Come on," Adam coaxed. "How about just her name? If it's this serious, I'll probably meet her soon enough."

His stomach dropped at the thought that he might never get to introduce Sam as his girlfriend, and he was surprised by how much he wished things were different. Though he knew there were many men who would've loved just sleeping with a beautiful, sexy woman without any commitments, he didn't—at least not with Sam. He wanted so much more than that. He would spend the rest of his life with her if he could.

"There's no one," he said, the words feeling like dust in his mouth.

He hated lying to his friend, but he'd promised Sam. He wondered if she would ever be willing to go public with their relationship before he shook off the thought. She was so worried about what other people would think of them and their relationship that they did their own dishes whenever he stayed at her place. She didn't even want her cook to find out that she was seeing anyone. He was dreaming if he thought that she'd ever be comfortable dating him publicly.

"So business is picking up?" Adam asked.

"You could say that," Luke averred. "It's definitely stabilizing. We've gotten back around a quarter of the business we've lost." As expected, it was mostly high net-worth individuals, but they did land one pension fund.

"That's good to hear. Hey, before I forget, can you give me Sam's number? Her old one's been disconnected."

Luke's blood froze. *Did Adam want Sam, too?* Was it possible Adam had fallen for her throughout the years as well? "What for?"

"What are you? Her bodyguard?" Adam laughed as he took another a gulp of his drink. "I need a date for Larry Thomas's wedding. You know how women are with weddings. They get all these ideas in their head and push for a proposal regardless of how long you've been dating. I would rather just have a nice, uncomplicated date who won't get any crazy ideas for once."

"Sure. I'll text you her number." *When pigs fly.* No matter how innocent Adam's intention may be, Luke didn't like the thought of Sam with another man. His insides twisted at the memory of how snugly her body had molded with his last night. He didn't want anyone touching her—in any way—except *him*. The fact that Sam had always been happy to see Adam whenever he'd visited the office cemented Luke's decision. He wasn't going to give him her number.

"Don't you have it on your phone?" Adam asked. "I was hoping to ask her today. The wedding's next Saturday."

Luke's jaw clenched. He'd been talking on the phone when he'd walked into the restaurant, so it wasn't as if he could say that he'd left his phone in his office then conveniently forget to call Adam. Unless he told the man about his and Sam's relationship, he was cornered.

He was about to tell Adam that Sam was taken before he remembered the vulnerability in Sam's eyes when she'd asked him to keep their fling a secret. She would've never agreed to a fling if he hadn't.

Knowing that he couldn't betray her, he got his phone from his coat pocket. His fingers were stiff as he swiped his phone's screen to get her number, and when he began reading it off, he practically had to force the information out of his throat. The temptation to give his friend one wrong digit was staggering, but he didn't need his friend questioning his actions even more.

"Thanks, man," Adam said as he clapped him on his back, and Luke wondered if he should try to warn Sam before Adam called.

But what if she actually wanted to go with him?

Luke's stomach dropped at the thought. No matter how much he'd tried to think otherwise, what they had was just a fling. Sooner or later, she'd end things and all he'd be left with were memories.

He couldn't help but think that he wouldn't have to worry if she'd been anyone else. His wealth was significant enough that he was considered "a catch." But not only did Sam have more money than she would ever need, she didn't care much for it unless it was in ways she could help other people with it. The only reason she was with him was probably because he was familiar, and she had some crazy notion that he was a better person than he really was. Sooner or later, she'd realize her mistake and end things, but hopefully, it would be later rather than sooner, because he was nowhere near getting his fill of her.

* * *

Sam smiled as she looked through all the pictures Cindy had emailed her from the private cooking class she'd won at the charity auction. It looked like her sister had fun.

Sam rolled her eyes when Cindy said that José Patron was even more handsome in person. Her sister had already mentioned that fact multiple times since the class. Sam was about to respond to Cindy's email when her phone rang. Her stomach dropped at the thought that it was Luke calling to say that he couldn't make it tonight. Though they spent most nights together, he sometimes had to cancel because he'd gotten held up at work.

Knowing that ignoring his call wouldn't change the fact that he couldn't make it, she picked up the phone.

"Hey," she answered, hoping her disappointment wasn't too obvious. No matter how much she hated it when he cancelled, she didn't want him to feel guilty about it either.

"Hey, Samantha." Surprise and relief coursed through her when she heard Adam's voice. *Luke wasn't calling to cancel on her.*

"Hi, Adam. How's everything going?"

"Good, although I'm hurt you changed your number without bothering to tell me. I had to get it from Luke."

Sam laughed. "I'm sorry. The press was hounding me

like crazy. I just needed it to stop." She knew the interest would've died eventually, but she hadn't wanted to wait.

"I know. I was just joking. How've things been going with you?"

"Good. I'm trying out my hand at investing."

"That must be…interesting."

A smile tugged at her lips. She knew how boring it must seem to other people that she spent her days poring over page after page of financial statements, but she thought it fun. It was like trying to find a needle in the haystack, except she occasionally struck gold.

"Maybe you could try it one day," she suggested. She'd never pictured herself investing until Luke had mentioned it and she found that she really enjoyed it. She didn't have to convince a portfolio manager to buy or sell a position, because she was the one in charge now.

"You know just as well as I do that Luke can manage my money better than I ever could, so I'll leave the investing to him and stick to buildings. Now, the reason I called was because I was wondering if you wanted to go with me to Larry Thomas's wedding next Saturday."

Sam froze. Hadn't he said that he'd gotten her number from Luke?

Did Luke know Adam was going to ask her out? Probably. It was unlikely Adam would just ask for her number without an explanation, which meant that Luke knew about this. Her stomach dropped. Was Luke seriously okay with her being Adam's wedding date? Though it was all probably innocent, she couldn't help but feel miffed that Luke didn't seem to care whether she went or not. She knew *she'd* be bothered if Luke accompanied another woman to a wedding.

The fact that he hadn't even blinked at her being someone else's date just showed that he wasn't serious about her. And though they'd made no commitments, she was hurt. Even if what they had was just temporary, he should only want her to be with him for the time being, right? He shouldn't be passing out her number to other men!

Cursing herself for her foolishness, she answered, "I already have plans." She hadn't really thought that Luke was starting to feel something more for her, had she? "But thank you for thinking of me."

Adam groaned. "Do you know how hard it is to find a sane date for a wedding?"

"I'm sure you'll find a replacement easily enough." Not only was Adam handsome, he was rich and had a fun sense of humor as well.

Adam sighed. "I don't know. Maybe I'll just go by myself. It's been getting harder and harder to date ever since Luke and I were included in that eligible bachelors list."

"You're not actually expecting me to feel sorry for you, are you?" Hell, Jason must have been jealous about Adam being on that list as well, she now realized.

At the time, when Jason had kept mentioning Luke being featured on the list, she'd written it off as him wanting to embarrass his friend. Luke had never liked the attention he got from the press and it was just like Jason to tease him. But she now knew that that had been a clue that

Jason had been unhappy with their marriage. If he hadn't married her, he would've been one of those "eligible bachelors" as well.

Perhaps the three of them—Jason, Luke, and Adam—were more alike than she'd ever imagined. No matter what Adam said, she knew that he enjoyed getting attention from the women and she was sure Luke did as well. Was it just an aberration that Jason had married her?

He'd gotten bored and restless with her quickly enough. Would the same happen with Luke? Was it happening already? Maybe that's why he'd been okay with giving Adam her number. In the back of her head, she realized that this was why she'd suggested a fling. She wouldn't have had to worry about other women if what she and Luke had was just temporary.

She hadn't counted on her falling for him and she was. Frighteningly so. She wouldn't have been so hurt that he didn't care about her going on a date with someone else if she wasn't.

Adam laughed. "No. I guess not, but it was worth a shot. Let me know if you change your mind."

Disappointment coursed through her as she hung up a few minutes later. She'd actually begun to really like Luke and thought he'd felt the same. But it turned out that she was, once again, wrong.

* * *

Luke's mind was in a whirr as he approached Sam's apartment door that night. It was a little earlier than he'd planned, but he hadn't been able to concentrate at the office. All he'd wanted to do was to see Sam.

He'd been itching to call her since he'd left the restaurant, but he hadn't known what to say. *Adam is calling to ask you out. You're going to say no, right?*

Luke hadn't even wanted to think of the possibility of her saying yes. He wished he had the right to tell her not to go with Adam, but they didn't have that kind of a relationship. She'd think he was overreaching, and he would be. Just because he'd tricked himself into thinking this fling was something more than it really was didn't make it true.

His chest tightened as he opened the door and saw Sam on the couch, looking at him over the edge of her eReader. How many more times would he get to come home to her before she decided she deserved better?

Worried that that time would come soon enough, he forced the thought out of his mind, walked over to her, and kissed her. Was it his imagination or was she not kissing him back? Shaking the thought off, he smiled as he sat next to her and settled her legs over his lap.

"What are you reading?" he asked. With her, he never knew what to expect. She could be reading anything from a biography of a president to a highlander romance.

She set her eReader down and tucked her hair behind her ear as she straightened. "Adam called, asking me if I wanted to go to a wedding as his date."

His heart sank. Was this how she was going to say that she couldn't see him next weekend? On top of hating the thought of her being with another man, he hated that their time together was being cut short. Weekends were the only chance they had to really spend any length of time with each other, and she was going to spend one with another man?

He gritted his teeth. "And what did you say?"

No matter how much he wished it otherwise, he knew he had no say in the situation. He'd only risk losing her if he tried to stop her and he wouldn't dare that.

"I said no."

Relief like he'd never known flooded through him. *Thank goodness.* He smiled as he leaned against the couch, feeling as though a weight had been lifted from him.

"I know it's petty of me, but I'm happy you're not going with him," he said as he began rubbing her feet.

Her eyes widened. "You are?"

He smiled sheepishly. "Yeah. Call me a caveman, but I don't like the thought of you in another man's arms."

She removed her legs from his. "Then why did you give my number to him?"

"What was I supposed to do? With us keeping this relationship a secret, I couldn't tell him to find another date when he asked for your number." Luke shrugged and gestured towards her. "Besides, I wasn't sure if you actually wanted to go to the wedding or if you wanted to see Adam."

"Oh."

He blinked in surprise as understanding dawned. "Wait. You thought I *wanted* you to go with Adam?"

"I don't know… After everything that's happened with Jason…" She sighed. "I just wanted to let you know that if you ever want to end things, you can let me know—no hard feelings."

How could she talk about them breaking up so calmly? How could she act as if what they had was nothing? Didn't she feel *anything* for him? The thought of her feeling nothing for him when she ended things was a sobering thought. Was he just wasting his time in trying to make her love him? No. She had to feel something for him. A bond as strong as theirs couldn't just be one-sided, could it?

"All right," he murmured, though he didn't ask her to do the same. He knew he'd be wrecked when she broke up with him. But since that was neither here nor now, he pushed the thoughts aside.

His chest ached at the thought of everything she'd been through. Hating that she'd been hurt, and grateful that they weren't ending things just yet, he kissed her. Her lips softened against his, and he groaned. So soft. He snaked his hand around her small waist and settled her onto his lap. They might not see eye to eye on their relationship, but at least they connected in bed.

His hands dipped beneath her shirt as he explored the silky skin underneath. He trailed a line of kisses down her throat before settling on that sweet spot he knew made her weak and suckled it. She moaned, and the sound went straight to his cock.

Greedy, he removed her shirt and felt his head lighten when he saw her bare breasts. He loved it when she didn't wear a bra. He cupped both breasts, one in each hand, and flicked his thumbs over her nipples. Power coursed through him as her eyes fluttered and she leaned towards him. He was the one doing this to her. He was the one who was making her feel this way. Not Jason. Not Adam—him. Drunk on the thought, he took one of the pert tips into his mouth.

As if she couldn't get enough of him, she ran her soft hands all over him and his grip around her tightened. He *loved* it when she touched him and hated the thought of her hands on anyone else.

She gasped when he bit her nipple. He grinned, then laved it, soothing it, before biting the sensitive nipple again. Her nails dug into his back as he moved towards her other nipple, giving it the same treatment. Her moans filled the air, going straight to his cock. Needing her now, he wrapped her legs around his waist and stood. She began unbuttoning his shirt as he captured her lips in a kiss.

She removed his shirt as they tumbled into bed seconds later and began running her hands over him. Knowing that he wouldn't last if she kept that up, he moved lower, leaving a trail of kisses down her sexy stomach as he removed her pants and panties. He sent a prayer of thanks when he found her wet. He couldn't wait any longer. He quickly shed his pants and boxers and joined her in bed.

He entered her, and the sweet sensation of being gripped by her made his head light. *So good. She felt so fucking good.* He moved in and out of her, letting himself get lost in the sensation. She groaned, and it was the sweetest sound he'd ever heard.

Her hair was spread out over the pillow, her eyes were glossed over, and her cheeks were flushed to a delectable red. The thought of another man seeing her like this, either in the past or in the future, had him suddenly seeing green.

"Say my name," he said as he pumped into her. Her eyes fluttered as she moaned, and he repeated it again. "Say my name, Sam."

"Luke," she finally said breathlessly.

Male satisfaction poured through him. He loved hearing his name on her lips.

"Again," he demanded as he pounded into her.

"Luke."

He wrapped a leg over his shoulder and moved deep inside her again. The sensation of being so deep inside of her made him dizzy. She must've felt the same, because she gasped as her nails bit into his back. "Luke."

Like a man on a mission, he moved faster. Soon, her muscles tightened around him and her sweet moans filled the air as he felt her spasms. "Luke. Luke."

Groaning, he buried his face into her shoulder and followed.

"Let's go somewhere this weekend," Luke said as they were cuddling a little later. "How about Martha's Vineyard? We could take the jet and hire a different pilot to keep it all under wraps."

Sam was on the verge of saying yes when she frowned. It was just so easy being with Luke and she knew that if she let things continue on as they were, she would soon find herself in love. It was why Adam's call earlier had messed her up so much. She'd thought she and Luke had a good thing going on and she hadn't been ready to stop.

"I'm actually going to help my sister out with a field trip," she suddenly decided. Her sister had complained about the lack of parents who'd signed up to supervise the field trip this weekend in her email today. Sam had thought about helping out but hadn't wanted to cut her time with Luke short.

But maybe some time away from him would do her some good. She needed to get her head on straight—to remind herself that there was more to life than just Luke, that what she had with him was just temporary—a fling. And perhaps to remind herself not to get so lost in someone again that she neglected her friends and family.

"I was going to tell you a while ago, but I forgot."

"Of course," he said, but she could almost feel his disappointment.

Guilt bit at her, but she shoved it ruthlessly away. She had to protect herself.

She smiled as she turned towards him. "Maybe next time?" She loved the idea of going somewhere with him. Maybe too much. "What were you thinking?"

His hold on her tightened. "Our own private cottage, walks along the beach, and sex. Lots and lots of sex."

"No clams?"

"I'll buy you a whole shack."

"Mmm… I like the sound of that." It sounded like the perfect getaway. She wished she could give in and say yes, but she couldn't afford to. She'd fallen for Luke and was dangerously close to losing herself in him.

She could already see herself dropping everything to be with him the way she had with Jason, because she wanted to spend all her time with him. But her friends and family deserved more than that and until she knew how to handle her priorities better, she couldn't take this next step with Luke.

"I know what else you like." His eyes darkened as he moved over her and she soon lost all train of thought.

─────────

CHAPTER EIGHTEEN

─────────

"I picked this flower for you. It's yellow like your dress."

Sam's heart softened as she bent down and took the sunflower the young girl was giving her. With ponytails and big eyes, the girl was just adorable.

"Thank you. It's beautiful."

The kid smiled shyly before going off to join the rest of her group in the scavenger hunt. Sam's chest tightened as she straightened and watched the children circle a tree before heading towards another one. Would she ever have children?

She'd always thought she would, but now she wasn't so sure. Since she didn't want a child of hers to grow up without two parents, she'd have to get married and she wasn't sure she ever wanted to go through *that* again.

Luke would make a good parent.

She inwardly groaned when she realized the direction of her thoughts. What they had was a fling. She'd be gravely disappointed if she began thinking about love and marriage. Though she knew Luke cared about her, she doubted it was anywhere near love and wasn't sure if it would ever be. Besides, he'd never talked about making things more permanent between them.

"Thanks so much for doing this again," Cindy said as she approached. "I swear, at least two fathers and a teacher signed up for the camp just because of you."

"Because of me?" Sam asked, surprised.

Cindy grinned. "You haven't noticed the men offering to carry your bag or to help pitch your tent?"

Sam groaned. "I thought they were just trying to make me feel welcomed, you know? Because I'm not a parent or a teacher." She felt so stupid.

"I'm sorry, Sam. I would've told them that you weren't interested, but I needed the help. The camping trip would've been cancelled if we didn't get enough adults signed on and the kids worked so hard on the fundraising. I didn't want to disappoint them. The men are still pigs though. Can you imagine—hitting on a woman just months after her husband dies? I can't believe—"

"I've started seeing someone," Sam admitted before Cindy went too far. It wasn't the best way to break the news, but she didn't want her sister thinking she was something she wasn't.

"You… Wait, you what?"

"I started seeing someone. It's not something that either of us planned, it just…" Not knowing what to say, she shrugged.

"Is it serious?" Cindy asked after a moment.

"I think I'm falling for him," Sam admitted. She'd

thought that she could keep her feelings in check, but she was doing an awful job of it.

"And the guy? Does he feel the same?"

She was about to say no when she remembered how much Luke had cut his hours at the office since he'd started seeing her. Harkin had always been Luke's priority and yet, he was willing to take time off to be with her. And not only that, she was probably the longest relationship he'd ever had.

"I know he feels something," Sam finally said. "I'm just not sure what."

"Oh, my goodness—it's Luke, isn't it?" Cindy asked as she grabbed Sam's wrist. "That's why you were saying all those nice things about him when we went to the show!" Surprised that Cindy had guessed correctly, Sam nodded, and Cindy continued, "I can't believe this. I mean, this is you. You don't jump from guy to guy. How did this happen? How long has it been going on?"

Sam was about to admit everything about Jason before she stopped. What would Cindy think of her? Their parents had always taught them that it was what was on the inside that mattered and yet, Sam had let herself be caught up in Jason and the glitz and the glamour of his world. Though she doubted her sister would judge her, she was ashamed— especially when she wasn't sure she would've ever realized how empty her life had become if she hadn't found Jason's phone and seen the texts. She'd like to think that she would've eventually, but she wasn't completely convinced.

"A few months."

"It must really be serious then. Doesn't he have a two-date maximum policy? And you," she said, pointing accusingly at her. "You never do anything less than serious. The shortest relationship you ever had was Ben, who you were with for two years."

Sam frowned at the realization that her sister was right. Had she just been fooling herself, thinking that she could have a fling? Or had that been her excuse to be with Luke?

"Not that that's a bad thing," Cindy quickly added. "You're just that type of a person."

"How do you feel about Luke?" Sam asked hesitantly, glad to finally be able to talk to someone about him. When she analyzed financials, she always listened to her gut, but at the end of the day, she had real numbers to back her up. She didn't have that luxury when it came to relationships. It was all gut and instincts, and look how well that turned out.

"Oh, no. I'm not getting into this."

"Please? I promise not to hold anything against you, and I definitely won't tell Luke." She wasn't even supposed to tell anyone about their relationship.

"Fine," her younger sister said as she crossed her arms. "I know you were always complaining about him, but he's always been nice to me. Not to mention that he's always been respectful to Mom and Dad."

Was that a dig about Jason? That he hadn't been as nice and respectful?

"He just seems real, you know? You don't feel as if he's putting on a show, though I sometimes did wonder. It seemed as if you were always saying something bad about him, but I could never see it in his behavior."

"I misjudged him," Sam admitted. She was still ashamed of how she'd called him a liar when, in fact, he'd been the best of friends.

"I'll say. I still can't believe—"

"Ms. Johnson! Ms. Johnson!" one of the children interrupted her. "We finished the list! We won!"

Sam looked and saw a group of children, including the girl who'd given her the flower, quickly running towards them. "We won!"

Cindy pointed at her. "This isn't over," she said before she turned towards the children. "Good job! Now, let's go check to make sure we have everything."

Even though Cindy's words slightly intimidated her, Sam was enormously relieved to have finally told someone about Luke. And not only that, her sister thought Luke was a decent man. That had to count for something.

* * *

"Did you see Ham's CEO being interviewed today?" Sam asked as she moved her cell phone to her other ear and settled into her chair a week later. "The man couldn't even meet the reporter's eyes."

Luke laughed. "I wouldn't be able to, either, if I were him. He doctored the financials for almost his entire run as CEO."

"I'm still surprised at how long it went undetected." There had been at least two analysts who'd issued warnings about the company a few years ago, but nothing had really happened until a well-known investor sounded the alarm after he'd shorted the stock.

"That's what happens when no one has the incentive to do the right thing. The management was pocketing their high salaries and the shareholders and the accountants were making bank."

"I know I should probably be immune to this by now, but sometimes the greed of these people really surprises me," Sam admitted. It wasn't like it was just the CEO's doing. The accountants and the auditors had been in on the scheme as well and as a former accountant, it really bothered her how some people could be bought.

"I know what you mean. These accounting firms are putting their names on the line to make just a little bit more money. It's like they've learned nothing from the whole Rixel scandal. Sorry, Sam. Sheila is flagging me. I'll see you tonight."

Sam smiled as she put the phone down and turned on her computer. Hopefully, she could finish the review of the oil company she'd started on this morning before Luke came over. There was a hardware chain in the Northeast she was hoping to look into tomorrow.

She was just writing an email to the investor relations department of the oil company about one of the items on their balance sheet an hour later when the doorbell rang.

"It's me," she heard Nina's voice.

Surprised, Sam stood and headed towards the door. Nina was usually at work this time of day. She glanced at the video screen by the door and saw her friend smiling and bobbing up and down, looking as if she were ready to burst. Bemused, Sam hurried.

"I'm engaged!" Nina said the moment Sam opened the door. Her friend beamed as she held her hand, showing her a ring with a big solitaire diamond in the middle. "Andrew proposed last night."

"Oh, my goodness. Congratulations!" Sam said as she hugged her friend.

"Thanks," Nina said as they broke apart. "I still can't believe it. His voice was really distant when he invited me over. I was worried he was going to break up with me, and then this!" She beamed as she held up her hand again. "It was so romantic," she continued as she walked into the apartment. "I went to his hotel room and there were flowers and candles and music..." As if still in a daze, Nina plopped down on the leather couch.

"I'm so happy for you!" Sam said as she joined her friend. And she was. There was no one she knew who deserved this more. Her friend had had some pretty shitty boyfriends. It was a relief she'd finally found a good one. Sam just wished she'd met the guy before he proposed. The fact that she hadn't drove home just how much she'd missed in letting herself get absorbed in Jason. Jason had still been alive when Nina had started seeing Andrew. If Sam hadn't given up their weekly dinners because of her busy schedule with Jason, she was sure she would've met Andrew by now.

"Let's go out and celebrate," she said, hoping to remedy the situation as soon as possible.

"I'm sorry, Sam, but I can't. I have to go pack. I was just so excited I had to tell you in person."

"Pack? Where are you going?" Her friend occasionally had to go out of town to meet with a client or to be near the courthouse. There were times it wasn't even all that far, but things could get so hectic sometimes that it just made more sense to stay in a hotel than to manage the commute to and from her apartment.

"Oh, no. This isn't a case. I'm going to Washington to meet his parents this weekend and then I'm coming back to put in my two weeks and then I'll be off for good."

"You're moving to Washington?" Sam asked, surprised. Though it wasn't Washington State, Washington, D.C. was still miles away. She wouldn't be seeing her friend as often as she'd hoped.

"Yeah. It's not like he could move here," Nina said, and Sam nodded understandingly. Andrew had a small metal fabrication company in D.C. It wouldn't make sense for him to move to New York. But still... Sam couldn't help but remember how happy Nina had been to get her promotion and now she was throwing it all away for a man?

In the back of her head, she knew that it was what had happened with Jason that was making her feel this way, and she forced the negative thoughts away. Just because *she'd* lost herself in marriage didn't mean that Nina would as well.

"I'm going to miss you," Sam said as she grabbed her friend's hand. At least she could visit her often. Now that she wasn't working at Harkin, she definitely had the time to.

"I'm going to miss you, too," Nina murmured as she hugged her. "It sucks. It feels like we just got back together and now this happened!"

"I'll make sure to visit you."

"Thanks, and you know that I'll visit you as often as I can." Nina looked at her watch, then stood. "Now, I really need to get going. Andrew is picking me up at three. I'll call you when I get back."

A niggling doubt crept into Sam's head as she closed the door. Though she was happy for her friend, she couldn't help but wonder if she would ever be as happy as Nina was. Surprisingly, she wasn't balking at the idea of marriage as she would've a few months ago, and she knew the reason for that was Luke.

He'd caught her unaware and she was beginning to suspect she wouldn't mind marriage if it was with Luke.

CHAPTER NINETEEN

Luke groaned as Sam nibbled his neck. He got a brief glimpse of her sexy smile as she pulled away before she trailed kisses down his chest, sending sparks of electricity coursing through him.

His head lightened at the direction she was heading. He loved it when she took him in her mouth. Her hands ran greedily over him, and he couldn't help but smile at the thought that she enjoyed his body as much as he enjoyed hers. He wanted the desire to be mutual, for her to want him as much as he wanted her.

She brushed against his hardness before she took him into her hand and stroked lightly. Her eyes met his and the mixture of lust and playfulness in them had him smiling. Knowing what she wanted, he started, "Please—"

"Luke!"

His heart stopped at the sound of his mother's voice. Sam froze, her eyes widening. Could his mom have worse timing? Though, admittedly, if his mom came to visit his apartment while he was there, there was a big chance he would be in bed with Sam. He bolted out of the bed and shut the door, making sure to lock it. He went back to Sam, at a loss for what to say.

"How do you turn this thing on?" he heard his father say and figured he was trying to turn on the television.

"Here." His brother's voice filled the air then the sound of a business channel came on before it was quickly changed into a sports one. Of course. Sunday football. Some things never changed.

"It's my parents, my brother, and possibly, my sister," he whispered to Sam. She started to dress, so he did the same. "I gave them access to the elevator."

"And they just come by unexpectedly?" she asked as she straightened and looked at him. "What if you have someone over?"

"It's not like I make it a habit of bringing women here," he said as he ran a hand through his hair. Not only did he not have the time, he'd always hated that sense of disgust that had filled him afterward. Though it wasn't as if he'd been hoping Sam would come around and see him as someone other than her husband's friend, he couldn't stop comparing the women to Sam and had always found them lacking.

"Besides, my parents usually call first," he continued. He groaned at the realization that they had, most likely, called, but since he'd turned off his cell phone and disconnected his apartment phone last night before Sam had come over, he hadn't gotten the calls.

"Come on," he murmured after he'd put his pants on. The faster they went out there, the faster he and Sam could get back to what they were doing.

"Wait. I can't go out there." She looked horrified at the prospect.

Frowning, he straightened. "What do you mean you—Oh." His stomach dropped at the realization that she didn't want to see his parents. They already knew her, but as Jason's wife—not as the woman he loved, and he was caught off guard by how much he wanted his family to know about them. His mom was always nagging him about meeting the right woman, and he knew his father wanted him settled down as well. He wished he could tell them that he had.

But had he?

He knew that Sam was the woman he wanted to spend the rest of his life with, but even after everything they've been through, she still insisted on keeping their relationship a secret. Doubt that she wasn't as committed to the relationship as he was surfaced before he pushed it back. He *would* make it work between them.

"I'm sorry," Sam said as she shook her head. "But you know how bad it would look for the both of us."

He understood where she was coming from, but he didn't give a damn. Hell, they weren't doing anything wrong. They were two uncommitted adults, enjoying each other's company.

Someone tried to open the door and panic filled Sam's eyes.

"I'm just getting dressed!" he yelled.

"All right. All right," he heard his mom say.

He sighed as he ran a hand through his hair. "Let me just see what they want. I'll be right back."

"No. You don't—"

Before she could say more, he left and found his two siblings and father yelling at the football game playing on the TV and his mom standing at the window, enjoying the apartment's view.

"Luke!" His sister stood from the couch and ran to give him a hug.

He smiled as he hugged Anna. "Hey, what are you all doing here?"

There was a warning look in his mom's eyes as she went to hug him. "We tried calling, but you weren't picking up." Her gaze moved behind him to his bedroom, and he knew he wasn't hiding anything from her. He wanted to tell her that it wasn't what she was thinking, but trying to explain would only lead to questions he couldn't answer, so he resisted.

Anna piped up. "Dad and Brian helped me move the old couch into my dorm."

Luke frowned. "Why didn't you get a mover?"

His brother laughed. "For a couch?"

"Yeah. For a couch." One of these days, he would have to remind Brian that their father wasn't as strong as he once was.

"Is he coming or not?" his dad asked from the couch, barely taking his eyes off the TV, and Luke sighed. His mom should've known better than to plan anything when a game was on.

"To what?" Luke asked as he looked at his mom.

Anna smiled. "Mom and Dad are taking us all out to brunch."

Guilt dug into him. His parents rarely came to this part of the city, and he hadn't even known that they were coming. But he couldn't go. He had to talk with Sam.

"I'm sorry, I can't go. Maybe next time?"

"Of course, honey," his mom said as she laid a hand on his shoulder. "And don't forget to come to dinner next week."

"Yeah. If he can get out of bed." His brother smirked as he looked at him and Luke resisted the urge to smack him.

"Very funny," he said as he walked them to the elevator.

"There better be a television at the restaurant," his dad said. "It was good seeing you, son."

As soon as the elevator doors closed behind his family, Luke headed towards the bedroom, where he found a fully dressed Sam getting something from her bag. Disappointment coursed through him when he saw that it was her car keys. She was leaving.

"I could've let myself out," she murmured as she turned around.

"I'm not going with them." He sighed as he ran a hand down his face. He knew he was going to regret this, but he couldn't stop himself. "I don't want to keep us a secret anymore." He wasn't some teenager hiding his first girlfriend from his parents. He was thirty-four years old, for goodness' sake. He shouldn't have to hide the woman he loved from his parents.

He watched as the muscles in Sam's throat tightened.

He knew it wasn't what she'd signed up for, but he couldn't fool himself any longer. He loved her and wanted to spend his life with her without all this subterfuge.

"We had a deal," she finally said, breaking the silence, and it felt as if a rug had been pulled out from under him. Even after all this time, she didn't care enough about him, enough about what they had, to tell people that they were together. He knew she felt *something* for him, but he was beginning to doubt if she'd ever feel something more for him.

"I know, and I'm sorry, but I'm tired of hiding," he said as he took her in his arms. He hoped he wasn't making a mistake. He didn't want to stop seeing her—he'd never been as happy as he was when he was with her, and he knew that he'd be devastated if she thought being with him wasn't worth it. "And I want my family to meet the woman who means so much to me."

"But we've already met."

"As Jason's wife. I want them to know how much you mean to me."

She was silent for a moment before she murmured, "I'll think about it."

It wasn't much, but he was grateful she hadn't immediately rejected the idea.

He smiled as he got the keys from her hand. "Now, you can't really be thinking about leaving, can you? I had the whole weekend planned out."

A smile curved on her lips. "Oh, did you, now?"

"I did, and you're wearing much too many clothes for

what I had in mind." She might not love him, but the one thing he knew for sure was that they connected in bed. It wasn't much to build on, but it was all he had, and he would use it for all it was worth.

* * *

Samantha watched as Luke expertly flipped a pancake the next day. He was wearing the white shirt he'd worn yesterday, and she couldn't help but wonder how much longer this fling of theirs would last if she continued to insist on keeping their relationship a secret.

He was doing so much to make sure that no one found out about them. He always had to keep a bag of his things in his car so that her cleaner wouldn't know that she'd started seeing someone; he had to drive himself to work every day so that his driver wouldn't know about them. He even helped her wash and dry all the pots and pans when they made a meal so that her cook wouldn't know that they'd been used.

Why was he putting up with all of this?

He could have any woman he wanted and yet, he was running through all these hoops for her. Guilt bit into her at the realization that he deserved so much better than what she was giving him. Perhaps she shouldn't have freaked out so much yesterday when his family had visited, but she'd panicked. Meeting them as Luke's girlfriend would've made the fling more real somehow and she'd been scared. She still was.

She could easily see herself falling in love with him and him not loving her back. Though their relationship was the longest one she'd ever seen him in, she knew that it was more because of the fact that they'd known each other for so long than him truly feeling something for her. Sure, he might be fooling himself now—he wouldn't be pushing her to out their relationship and he wouldn't be spending so much time with her if he wasn't, but the novelty would eventually wear off and then where would that leave her?

But at the same time, she didn't want to let her fear of what other people thought of her make her lose him. She loved being with him and didn't want their relationship to end.

"I'd love to see your family again," she said before she lost her nerve, quickly adding, "if you're still interested."

Hadn't she felt relieved to be able to talk to Cindy about Luke? Luke probably just wanted the same thing.

He quickly turned towards her then, as if remembering the stove, he turned around and shut it off. "Of course, I'm still interested. The family's getting together at my parents' house next Saturday. Are you available?"

"Yeah."

"Great. I'll let my mom know. Thanks, Sam. This really means a lot to me."

She was suddenly glad that she could do something for him. He was always doing things for her and it was nice to finally be able to do something for him as well. And though she was still worried about what his family would think of her, she was also happy at the thought that Luke cared enough about her to introduce her to them—especially since she knew how important they were to him. It was a sign that this was more than just a fling, right?

Boy, she sure hoped so.

* * *

Excitement coursed through Luke as he dialed his mom's number on his way to his car an hour later.

"Luke? Is everything all right?"

It was only then that he realized the time. No wonder his mother was worried. It wasn't even seven in the morning yet. But he'd been excited to tell his parents about Sam.

"Yeah. Sorry, Mom. I just wanted to tell you that I'm going to bring someone next Saturday."

"Oh?"

"It's Sam," he quickly said, hating the censure in his mom's voice. After yesterday, he understood that. They probably thought that the woman in his bedroom was someone he'd just picked up at a party. But it wasn't like that at all.

"*Oh.*"

The inflection in his mom's voice told him exactly what she was thinking. Sam was still Jason's widow not only to his family, but to everyone they knew. They'd think that she was moving on too fast, and perhaps, that he was taking advantage of a broken-hearted widow.

It wasn't as if they knew Jason had been cheating on Sam for as long as the two of them had been married.

When his mom remained silent, Luke continued, "It's

not something either of us set out for. It just happened." Hell, maybe Sam had been right about keeping them a secret. But he was sick of hiding. He'd wanted to be with her for so long, and now that he was, he wanted to shout it from the top of his lungs.

"Of course, dear. You don't have to explain anything to us. We all knew how devastated the both of you were when Jason died. It makes sense that you two found comfort in each other."

"That's not—" he began, but stopped. He wanted to protest the idea that he and Sam had come together over a combined grief of losing Jason, but what could he say? That he'd wanted her to leave Jason for years? That definitely wouldn't get him any brownie points with his mom.

"Look, I know that it's not any of my business, but I just don't want either of you two to get hurt. Sam's already been through so much."

It was clear his mom thought that Sam was the injured party here, but he didn't know what to say to make her think differently.

"I'm not going to hurt her, Mom," he finally said.

"I know you don't mean to." His mom paused before sighing. "I just hope you two know what you're doing."

Luke was frowning by the end of the call. His mom was always bugging him to settle down and when he finally cared enough about a woman to bring her home, his mom was disappointed in him?

Great. That was just fucking great.

* * *

George was in *way* over his head with Clayton.

Luke frowned as he read the manager's report later that day. George wanted to buy into a small mortgage company in Nevada who'd approached them about selling some of their shares at a steep discount. The firm had had a higher number of defaults than expected and needed a new line of credit.

Sure, it was unlikely that they would file bankruptcy, but to pour twenty million into them? It was a risk Harkin simply couldn't afford right now. Luke reached for his phone, then hesitated. He and George had always had a difference of opinion about the way they diversified their portfolio. Luke preferred to invest a small amount in various companies while George liked to go big on just a few.

George felt as if there were only a limited number of good opportunities out there and liked to seize them with both hands whenever they came by. Luke was more cautious, believing that no matter how good they were at analyzing annual reports and businesses, there was always a possibility for error.

Neither of their approaches was wrong. At the end of the day, it all boiled down to their personal preferences. Luke shouldn't have expected George's strategy to change once he'd chosen him to head the distressed fund. Especially since George's instincts were one of the reasons he'd chosen him over Peter.

Luke wouldn't question the man—at least for now. He'd already done that many times in the seven years they'd worked together. George wouldn't have done this if he wasn't sure. Remembering just how much due diligence the man had put into that Oakbridge deal last year, Luke knew he had nothing to worry about. George had even caught things he hadn't seen. Luke spent a few more minutes looking over the rest of the report and was about to call George when his cell phone rang.

He grabbed it and saw his brother's name flash on the screen. He guessed his mom had just finished talking to Brian.

"Mom told you," Luke said in lieu of a greeting. He hoped his family didn't make this thing between him and Sam a big deal in front of her next Saturday, or she'd regret coming.

"Yeah. She asked if I knew anything about it. How long has it been going on?"

"Almost three months."

There was a pause before Brian asked, "It's her, isn't? She's the reason you never got serious about anyone. You were too caught up in her to notice anyone else."

"It wasn't like I was holding out for her."

Except for the brief moment of insanity when he'd thought he could get her to leave Jason, he'd always known that she would never leave Jason for him. He'd tried to get over her so many times—he'd seen other people, buried himself in work, and had even tried avoiding her, but it hadn't worked. Even getting a glimpse of her was more exciting than a date with someone else.

"Hey, I understand. You can't decide who you fall in

love with, though I finally understand that glare you were giving me at the Christmas party."

Luke winced as he remembered his reaction when he'd seen Sam laughing and dancing in his brother's arms at last year's company Christmas party. Though he knew she wouldn't have refused if he'd asked her to dance—no matter what she felt about him, she wouldn't publicly embarrass him—he'd been afraid of his lack of self-control. He'd feared that once he'd gotten her in his arms, he'd never want to let go. So, instead, he'd watched from the sidelines as she'd danced with Jason as well as a few others at the party, probably glaring at everyone she danced with —all the while wishing it were him.

"Was I that obvious?"

Brian laughed. "I didn't know what had changed. One minute, you were happy to see me, and the next, you looked like you wanted to castrate me."

Knowing just how close his brother was to the truth, Luke winced.

"So, do I have to start preparing a best man speech?"

Luke's chest tightened. There was nothing he wanted more than to marry Sam, but he doubted she felt the same. Sure, she was willing to meet his parents as his girlfriend, but one dinner wasn't anywhere near the vicinity of marriage.

Not wanting to think about just how far the possibility of marriage was for them, he asked, "What makes you think I'd choose you?"

"Why wouldn't you? You can't possibly be thinking about choosing Adam over me. I'm your brother."

"He's definitely the safer choice," Luke teased. "I wouldn't have to worry about him showing any embarrassing baby pictures." Luke doubted he'd ever forget how red Anna's cheeks had become when Brian had brought out the baby pictures the first time she'd ever brought home a boyfriend.

"How about just one?"

Luke laughed. He couldn't believe his brother was trying to negotiate.

Brian's voice sobered. "You are going to marry her, aren't you?"

"It's a little too soon to be thinking about that," Luke admitted. "Sam doesn't even want other people to know about us."

"But isn't that understandable to want a little privacy? I mean, the news of the two of you dating, especially so soon after Jason's death, would definitely make it to the front of the tabloids. And besides, she let you tell us about the relationship, didn't she?"

"Yeah." After he'd practically forced her hand. Considering his mom's response, he wondered if he'd been wrong to force the issue. It certainly wouldn't help his cause if the first people they saw as a couple didn't approve of their relationship. Sam might not want to risk the censure a second time.

Hell. He hoped he hadn't messed things up by pushing her to meet his parents.

He should've just been content to be with her and to take whatever she'd been willing to give, but he hadn't been able to stop himself. After loving her for so long, he wanted everything.

His stomach twisted at the thought that he could've screwed up the best thing that had ever happened to him and he suddenly didn't feel like talking about it.

"I'm sorry, Brian. Can I call you back?"

CHAPTER TWENTY

"So…are we going to your childhood home?" Sam asked as they got on the highway Saturday evening, heading toward his parents' house.

Luke glanced at her before returning his attention to the road. "No. I got my parents to move out a few years ago."

"You're lucky you got them to move. All my parents let me do was install a security system for them." She'd tried to give her parents money to move so many times, but they'd always refused.

She understood that the house had taken them thirty years to pay off and that it was their pride and joy, but she wished they'd let her do more for them. But they'd even refused her offers to fix the little things like the wobbly porch steps and the tattered couch her dad loved so much.

"Bad neighborhood?"

She hesitated before answering. "It's so-so," she finally said, knowing that while it could be a lot better, it could also be a lot worse. "They have some good neighbors and some shady ones as well." She shrugged. "I guess I just want something better for them."

Like a house with stairs that didn't creak and a neighborhood where she wouldn't have to worry about drive-by shootings.

"I know what you mean," Luke told her. "I wanted something with gates, or at least, a house in a gated community, but my parents were having none of that. They didn't want to alienate their old friends."

"Yeah. My parents were never comfortable with Jason's lifestyle, either. Even going out to eat was a chore for them."

Luke laughed. "I can just imagine. Jason was always into the hottest new restaurants. I swear, one of the restaurants he brought me to served raw food. And I'm not talking about sushi."

"It's supposed to have more nutrients," Sam said, laughing.

"That may be, but I'm not eating beef that hasn't been cooked."

Sam smiled as she gestured towards him. "You already know how I feel about some of those places. I think I've gained twenty pounds from eating all the food that I've missed over the years."

"Hmm…remind me to look for those twenty pounds later on. I haven't seen them, but perhaps I haven't been looking close enough."

He gave her a rakish smile, and heat spread through her face at the thought of him inspecting her. She was positive he knew every inch of her, but it couldn't hurt to check.

* * *

"It's sweet that you got them a new place," Sam said as she got the box of chocolates out of his trunk twenty minutes later. Luke's heart swelled as he remembered her asking if his parents liked chocolate. It showed that she wanted to make an impression on his parents, and he hoped it meant that she was falling for him.

"I'm sure you would've done the same if you were in my shoes," he said as he got the ice cream then closed the trunk.

"Hey, do you need help?" Anna called out as she approached them. She was staying home for spring break.

"No. We're good. Thanks."

"Hey, Sam!" Anna beamed as she hugged Sam.

"Hey, Anna, long time no see."

"I know! I've been so busy with school that I haven't had time to visit the office."

Luke was surprised that Anna saw Sam when she visited him at the office, but he shouldn't have been. Sam was friends with *everyone*. Anna smiled as she hugged him.

"Hey, Diana," Sam said and he looked up to see Sam hugging his mom. "I brought you and Richard some chocolates."

"Aww… Thank you, dear. You didn't have to do that."

"It's nothing. Do you need any help in the kitchen?"

Knowing how much Sam hated cooking, Luke felt his heart soften at the thought of her willing to help his mom and just about become a puddle when his mom accepted

Sam's offer. His mom only allowed people that she liked in her kitchen.

"Let me just put the ice cream in the freezer," he said, and his mom waved him off.

"I'll get it," she said as she took it from him and hugged him. "I think your brother wants to talk with you," she said softly.

Curious, he nodded and watched as the three most important women in his life walked into the house, laughing. The weight that he'd felt ever since his call with his mom lifted as he followed them into the house.

His brother quickly stepped into view. Brian tilted his head towards the kitchen.

"She looks happy," his brother said. "You do, too."

"I really am." He just hoped he made Sam half as happy as she made him.

Brian flashed him a smile. "Do you want to see something cool?"

"Sure."

His brother nodded at something behind him. Luke turned around and noticed the new wooden blinds. Surprised, he walked towards them.

"Dad made them," Brian continued behind him and Luke turned, surprised.

"Dad *made* this?" Luke asked as he opened and closed the blinds, admiring his dad's handiwork. It looked like something from a catalogue.

"Yeah. He said he was getting bored with retirement."

Luke opened and closed the blinds again—he hadn't known that Dad was so talented. Though Dad had always fixed things around the house, Luke had thought it was because they couldn't afford a handyman. Was it possible Dad had done the work because he'd enjoyed it?

"Do you want to see what he's doing with the extra wood?"

"Please don't tell me that he's redoing the floors." *That had to be too much work for Dad.* Though he was glad his father had found something to do with his time, Luke didn't want him to be overtaxed. He'd earned his retirement.

"Nope." Brian grinned. "I'll show you."

"All right. Lead the way." As they made their way towards the basement, Luke asked, "So, how's everything?"

"It could be better." Brian sighed and shook his head. "I think I'm just burnt out. To be honest, I never thought that I'd stay at the bank this long."

It must be a family thing to never look for a better job. Both of their parents had retired from the first jobs they'd ever had. The jobs weren't the best, but he guessed that they'd felt lucky just to have a job, and it seemed he and his siblings had inherited the same trait. He himself would've still been at Brown and Hale if it wasn't for Jason. He'd been content at the chance of a better life, not knowing that there was a whole other world out there just within his grasp.

"The offer for a loan is still available if you ever decide to pursue something else." Brian had always been the creative one in the family. He'd used to drive Mom crazy when he took things in the house apart to make his own gadgets.

Luke had always thought his brother would become an engineer or an inventor, so he'd been surprised when Brian had gotten a job at a local bank right after graduation.

"Thanks. I'll think about it. Sometimes I think I'm just jealous when I see all the fun Dad is having woodworking." Brian opened the basement door and the smell of wood hit Luke.

"Oh, is it time for dinner, already?" his dad asked as he stopped hammering.

"Almost," Brian answered as they went down the stairs. "Mom hasn't said anything yet."

Luke looked at the rough sketch on the table. His dad wasn't as good at drawing as he was at woodworking, but Luke could see that this was going to be a beautiful bird house.

"It's going to be my anniversary present to your mother," Dad said.

"Mom's going to love it," Luke said with a smile. Mom had always had a fondness for animals. And while he was happy that his father was doing something that he clearly enjoyed, he hated that his dad had to wait until he was already retired before he got to do the things he wanted. Dad had never even gone on a vacation until last year when he and Mom had done a cruise in Europe. They'd enjoyed it so much that they'd booked another cruise within a week of coming back home.

It was strange to think about how his parents had never had the money for these type of luxuries when he'd been younger—they'd always just had enough—and how he now had the money to do just about anything he wanted, but not the time and he realized that that had to change if he wanted a family with Sam. And he did. He wanted everything with her—the house in the suburbs, children… But at the same time, he didn't want to be like his dad, who'd always come home too exhausted to play catch or to help with homework.

Though he knew that his father had done the best that he could, under the circumstances, he also knew that he was in a different place in life than his dad had been. He *could* step back from work without suffering financially, and he would when he and Sam had children, he suddenly decided. He didn't want to end up like his father, who'd only gotten to enjoy life after he'd retired—especially when he had a choice.

* * *

"Thanks so much for coming with me tonight," Luke said as the elevator doors opened to his apartment.

"I think that's the fourth time you thanked me."

Luke smiled as he took her in his arms. "I'm just really happy."

Pleasure filled her at the thought that something as simple as her accompanying him to his family dinner could make him so happy.

From Luke's mom, she knew that she was the first woman he'd ever brought home. A big part of her was thrilled at the thought. She loved being with Luke and was glad he felt something with her that he hadn't felt with anyone else. But another, more rational part of her worried that things were moving too fast. She'd literally found out that her husband had been cheating minutes before jumping into bed with Luke and now she was going to his family dinners?

Luke's arms tightened around her. "Dance with me?" he asked as he swayed her.

She laughed as she wrapped her arms around him. "There's no music."

"I got it right here," he said as he took his cell phone out. With his eyes on her, he asked the phone for smooth music then tossed it on the couch. Soon, the sound of a saxophone filled the room. He smiled as he wrapped his arms around her again. "Now, where were we?"

"Hmm…you were saying how you were going to make me your famous pecan waffles in the morning as a thank-you for going to your parents' tonight."

"Was I?"

She grabbed his butt and felt his hardness against her belly. "Among other things."

"Oh, you'll get your waffles," he murmured as he bent his head and ran his tongue over her ear, sending shivers down her spine. "Among other things," he continued before he kissed her.

CHAPTER TWENTY-ONE

Insane. He was definitely insane.

One dinner with Sam and he was already picking out rings? She wasn't even ready to tell people that they were seeing each other.

But even with that knowledge, Luke typed his credit card information into the website where he'd just spent the last two hours designing a ring for Sam. Somehow, he'd gone from reading a report about a mining company to looking for a wedding ring. After not finding anything worthy of her at the main jewelers, he'd ended up on a site that allowed him to design the perfect ring.

He'd played with a lot of settings and stones before deciding on a simple platinum ring with a flawless princess-cut diamond in the middle. It wasn't the big diamond she deserved, but he knew that she would never like anything that was flashy or gaudy. Besides, he didn't want her to feel uncomfortable wearing it. In fact, he wanted her to wear it everywhere she went.

Satisfaction coursed through him at the thought of her wearing his ring before reality set in. Going to a family dinner with him had definitely been a move in the right direction, but it was still far, far, far away from marriage. Hell, he couldn't even get her to agree to a date out in public where they might be seen by people they know. How was he going to get her to spend the rest of her life with him?

He ran a hand through his hair in frustration. He knew that she'd been through a lot with Jason, and it was understandable that she wanted to control the boundaries of their relationship. But he *hated* that he only got to spend nights and mornings with her. He wanted so much more. He wanted to take her out on dates and to see her throughout the day. He wanted it to be okay to call her and to have someone know who he was talking to. After being used to having her at the office, he missed being able to step out of his office and seeing her in hers. And not only that, he wanted to live with her. He wanted to come home to her every day and wanted to be the one she came home to every day as well. And because of that, he continued with the transaction.

He didn't even know her size.

He would've laughed if it wasn't so depressing. If Nina had known that they were seeing each other, he could've asked her for help. But Sam hadn't even confided in her best friend about them. And he was not going to borrow her old wedding ring to check its size, even though he knew exactly where it was. He didn't want something so special to be tainted by her relationship with Jason.

But for some odd reason, Luke thought she was a five. He didn't have any experience with rings, but he felt it in his bones. Besides, he could have the ring adjusted if it was the wrong size.

He pushed aside the doubts that were crowding in. However impulsive purchasing this ring was, it was the right thing to do. She was the only person he could ever imagine spending the rest of his life with. And when he finally had the chance to ask her to marry him? Well, he'd worry about her answer then.

* * *

"We're expecting the competition in the toy industry to be fiercer in the years to come," George told him. "Toyco's market share has been steadily increasing and Playtime has just signed a licensing deal with Juniper."

"Juniper is the company who's been doing all those superhero movies?" Luke clarified. He was pretty sure he'd seen the commercials.

"Yeah. They just released *The Menagerie* in November and their upcoming *Bearman* film is expected to be a huge hit."

Luke nodded and looked over Seidler's financials. The distressed fund had owned the company's stock for almost two years and had made a decent amount of return. The financials were still strong—even stronger than when they'd first bought them—but they were just facing too many headwinds. A new line of toys coming up or new additions to their current lines might've helped, but they didn't have those. Not even plans to develop them in the near future.

He flipped through the financials and frowned when he saw that the company had started buying back their stock. Though buying back stock often added value to a company, Luke didn't like it here. There was still room for growth in the company and instead of doing that, they'd chosen to remain stagnant.

Henry, one of the analysts, began talking about how their strong earnings last quarter made it the best time to sell their position in the company, and Luke found himself mentally agreeing.

Suddenly, the air suddenly changed. He turned and saw Samantha talking to one of the lawyers near the coffee station. As if sensing him watching her, she turned and smiled at him before returning to her conversation. His heart beat faster as he turned back towards the financials. *What was she doing here?* Had she come to see him? Knowing that George and the analysts had already done their due diligence before approaching him about selling the stock, he nodded at them. "Sell it all."

The group quickly disassembled, and Luke headed out to meet Sam. She was now talking to Karen and he couldn't help but think about how right it was to have Sam back at the office. She *belonged* here.

Karen laughed at something Sam said and Sam joined in. His heart skipped a beat as their gazes met. Even after they'd been in each other's pockets for months, she still made his heart stop at the sight of her. She smiled, and he couldn't help but feel pride at the thought that the smile was for him alone. It was petty of him, but he was really glad that it was finally him and not Jason she was sharing her smiles with.

Noticing that Sam's attention was elsewhere, Karen turned and saw him.

"Uh-oh," she said as she turned towards Sam and touched her arm. "I better get back to my desk before the two of you come to blows. It was nice seeing you."

Luke's first instinct was to hug and kiss Sam, the way he always did when he saw her, but Karen's words gave him pause. They were in public, and Sam hadn't said that she was willing to out their relationship and so, he stuck his hands in his pockets.

"Hey, Sam."

"Hey, Luke," she said as she tightened the grip on her bag. "I just wanted to see if you were free for lunch."

She wanted to take him out to lunch?

He couldn't move fast enough. "Sure. Just give me a minute." It was almost too good to be true. First, he'd been hoping that she'd be more comfortable with their relationship, and now she was here.

He went to Sheila and made sure that there was nothing urgent he had to do in the next hour, then told her that he was going out. By the time he returned to the trading floor, Sam was talking to Cecilia.

Cecilia noticed him as he approached them and quickly moved her mouse to close the window on her computer. His lips twitched. It wasn't as if he didn't know that the accountant showed pictures of her nieces and nephews to anyone that would look at them. Her voice was so loud that he would often hear her from across the floor.

But since she didn't want to be caught, he chose not to comment on it and suddenly wondered if Sam would be just as eager to show everyone pictures of their children. His chest tightened at the thought. He'd never really imagined himself as a family man, but he found himself wanting a family with Sam. Hell. Even the suburbs were starting to sound good as long as she was there with him.

"You ready?" he asked as he approached her. The urge to wrap his arm around her waist and kiss her was overwhelming, but he resisted. He didn't want to make her regret inviting him to lunch.

Sam nodded then said goodbye to Cecilia. He didn't miss the way the accountant beamed as she turned back to her computer. Sam had that effect on people.

"You know the door's always open if you want to come back," he said as they headed toward the elevator. She froze, so he rushed to explain. "You're already doing the work. You might as well do it here. You can even have the other guys analyze the companies you don't want to do. Who knows? Maybe they even did it already. I'm sure that there's some overlap between the companies you're looking into and the ones the guys are doing here. We could set aside a portion of a fund for you to manage—"

"I—that's—" She shook her head. "I really appreciate the offer, but I can't."

His stomach dropped. Did she not want to spend all her time with him the way he did with her? He'd hoped her surprising him at the office was a sign that she'd begun to miss him during the day, but perhaps he'd been wrong.

Did she not think that they were going to last? Was that why she was refusing to let their relationship be known and why she'd refused his offer? She didn't want to make things awkward between the two of them when things ended?

Because he was just offering her to do the same thing she was already doing at home, but around the people he knew she loved to work with and she wasn't having any of it. Trying not to let the hurt dig into him, he changed topics as they began walking again. At least she was here. That was something.

"She's always been so skittish around me," he said, indicating Cecilia with a motion of his head.

"Who? Cecilia?"

"Yeah. At first, I thought it was because I was the boss, but then I saw how normal she acted around Jason."

Sam laughed. "That's because Jason was practically harmless. You, on the other hand, can be downright frightening at times. I don't know if you've noticed or not, but almost everyone here has been wary of you at one point or another."

"Even you?" he asked, surprised.

"*Especially* me. I'll admit that there were times I thought I wouldn't last at the company—especially during those first few months. You just always seemed so angry at me." She shrugged as she turned towards him. "I know you never wanted me working here in the first place."

He winced at the memory of how against he'd been about her working at the company. He hadn't even tried to hide how wrong he thought her for the job, but Jason had persisted and for that Luke was grateful. He'd never have these past months with Sam if Jason hadn't insisted on her working there.

"I'm sorry, Sam. I should've given you a chance." It was ironic how much he'd wanted her gone initially when he was willing to do just about anything for her to come back now.

"I probably would've felt the same if I'd been in your shoes," she said as they walked into the private elevator. "I had no experience with these kinds of things, and my accounting background barely helped. It's a whole other world here."

But she'd learn quickly and had made him eat every single one of his words. The elevator doors closed, and he reached for her arm. "I'm really sorry for whatever pain I caused you."

"It's all right. I guess we're even now."

Laughing, he had the sudden urge to kiss her. He was about to pull her to him when he remembered the cameras in the elevator and let go. Tonight, he promised himself. Tonight, he'd kiss and touch her to his heart's desire.

* * *

"Thank you for lunch," Sam said as they rode the private elevator to the office an hour and a half later. She knew that she should've left when they'd reached the door of the building, but she was having too much fun and didn't want to leave just yet.

Luke smiled and the warmth of it spread through her. "Any time."

She was just wondering if tomorrow would be too soon when the elevator doors opened. Theresa bolted from her chair the moment she saw them. "Luke, George has been looking for you."

"Thanks," he murmured to the receptionist as he walked unhurriedly towards the glass door leading to the trading floor and opened it for Sam.

As soon as they walked onto the floor, she heard George's voice. "I've been trying to reach your cell."

George jogged over with a bunch of papers in his hand. "I need you to sign these," George said as he handed them to Luke.

Seeing that Luke was busy, Sam smiled. "I'll see you later."

Appreciation shone in his eyes. "Thanks." He turned towards George and took the pen the manager was handing him.

"Trade sheets?" Luke asked George as he began signing them on the wall.

Knowing how busy Luke was, Sam was touched that he'd been okay with taking her out to lunch and couldn't help but remember the way he'd offered to take her out to lunch after their first weekend together. In all the years that they'd worked together, he rarely went out to lunch—let alone for a woman. He didn't like any distraction during working hours. And yet, he'd been willing to go with her. Though she tried to tell herself that it didn't mean anything, she found herself grinning as she pulled out her phone to tell Charles to start the car.

She was just about to hit the dial button when she noticed Jason's room was half-lit. Knowing that she'd never really said goodbye, she put her phone in her bag and approached it. Janet wasn't at her desk. From Luke, Sam knew that Jason's assistant had been transferred to the client relations department a few weeks earlier and was doing a wonderful job.

Sam flipped on the other light switch as she walked into the familiar room. Everything—from his little golf set up on the right to the pictures of him with various politicians was exactly in the same condition as he'd left it in. The only clue someone would've had that he wasn't on some business trip were the white boxes on the floor and on his desk. She guessed that Janet had taken the files out of his desk and cabinet in case someone needed them.

Sam frowned as she went over and sat on the leather couch at the back of the room. *Nothing*. She felt absolutely nothing. She'd thought she'd feel something more when she walked in. Maybe anger at the way Jason had thrown away their marriage or frustration over the years she'd wasted with him, but she didn't even begrudge him that. Because if it wasn't for him, she would've never met Luke and would've never had these amazing past few months.

Luke.

Her chest tightened at the realization that it was because of him that she was no longer angry at Jason. She was just so happy that she didn't have it in her to be anything but happy. It was still no excuse for Jason cheating on her, but she could understand it a bit more if he'd felt even an ounce of what she felt when she was with Luke. She'd certainly never felt that way with Jason.

Her heart leapt at the realization that she loved Luke. In a much bigger way than she'd ever loved Jason. She wasn't even sure now if what she'd felt for Jason was love or not. Those emotions seemed like such a pale comparison to what she felt for Luke and she couldn't help but think that what she'd had with Jason was puppy love and what she had for Luke was a full-fledged love.

She'd tell Luke tonight, she quickly decided.

Though he might not feel the same about her as she did him, she wanted him to know that she loved him. He deserved at least that after he'd helped her through so much. She would've probably spent these past few months angry and hurt, stuck in the same emotional rut if it hadn't been for him. Her heart suddenly felt free and light as she stood and turned the lights off.

Goodbye, Jason.

"I need you to sign these," George said as he passed him a bunch of papers.

Luke frowned. "Trade sheets?"

"I'll see you later," Sam said.

Luke sighed as he turned towards her. He'd been hoping to get some alone time with her, but he guessed he'd have to wait for tonight. "Thanks." She was always so considerate about his work. He took the pen George was offering and began signing the authorization sheets.

"Olson's sliced their dividend in half after they missed their estimated earnings. They're blaming the storm," George said wryly.

Luke inwardly shook his head as he handed the papers back to George. They knew it wasn't the storm, because all the other department stores were having record years. They'd known Olson's was struggling when they'd first bought it, but they'd seen potential in the retailer's turn-around plan. But when the revamped stores turned out to be more of the same old, same old, they'd slowly began selling their shares. The dividend cut was the last straw.

Luke pulled up the company on his phone as soon as George left. The stock price had dropped more than a quarter since the announcement. Shaking his head, he headed towards his office to look up their latest report.

He was recalculating the free cash flow in his office twenty minutes later when George walked in.

"We were able to get rid of everything at a twenty percent loss." There was a pause before George added, "I couldn't get ahold of you."

Luke winced at the realization that he'd kept his phone off since last night. "I'm sorry." George had the authority to do smaller trades, but anything larger than ten million required Luke's approval.

His first instinct was to raise the maximum amounts his managers could do without his approval before guilt set in. The problem wasn't with the limits his managers had to work with. The problem was with him. He'd been taking a lot of time off work to spend with Sam—often leaving early at night and coming in late as well. To top it all off, he was probably only doing a tenth of the work he'd used to do at home. So, no, raising the maximum so that he wouldn't always have to be by a phone wasn't the answer. A maximum of ten million for a single trade was big enough as it was. He simply shouldn't have turned off his phone.

He was lucky it was only this and not something big like another accounting scandal. His guilt intensified at the knowledge he hadn't been doing the extra round of due diligence he'd always done before. Instead, he'd been relying more and more on the reports the analysts and managers made.

And even though their team was one of the best in the business, they sometimes made mistakes. His review had always been that extra safeguard. His stomach hollowed at the realization of how damaging this setback could've been if it had been bigger. After everything that they'd been through, it would've destroyed Harkin.

George let out a huge sigh as he settled into the chair across from him, his shoulders defeated. "Are you planning on closing the company?"

"What? No. What makes you say that?"

George gestured towards him. "You've been out of it these past couple of weeks—coming to work late, leaving early…"

The memory of how quickly he'd okayed the sale of their Seidler shares as soon as he'd seen Sam needled him. He'd just wanted to get out of there as quickly as possible.

Had he seriously just risked the company's future for a

woman who didn't even want to let people know that she was with him? He inwardly groaned as he thought about his plans to lessen his workload when they had kids so that he could spend more time with them and Sam.

"I'm sorry, George. I won't let something like this happen again."

He had a responsibility not only to himself, but to his employees and to his investors. His carelessness could cost a pensioner his timely retirement the same way the hedge fund who'd handled his father's pension had ruined his. The thought alone set Luke's priorities and focus straight. He couldn't let them, any of them, down again.

CHAPTER TWENTY-TWO

Sam was brimming with excitement as she prepared the table. The realization that she loved Luke had come with the epiphany that she didn't want to hold anything back anymore.

In fact, she wanted everything with him. Love, family, marriage... All those dreams she'd thought had died had come back with a startling force, and she hoped that he wanted the same thing. Though she'd save talk of marriage and family for another time, she'd tell him that she loved him and that she didn't want to keep their relationship a secret anymore.

She now knew that the latter had been the coward's way out. It was as if she'd always had one foot out the door—as if she'd thought that their relationship wouldn't last. But ever since she'd decided to tell Luke about her feelings, a sense of calmness seemed to have settled over her and she'd stopped worrying about the fall out of their relationship, because she knew Luke would catch her and she, him.

She straightened and looked at her work. The table looked perfect. For decorations, she'd added a fresh pot of roses as well as matching candles on both sides. She had the wine chilling, the salad and cake in the refrigerator, and the rest of the food was in the oven warming. She was just about to go change into the new black dress she'd bought when her cell phone chimed. She picked it up and felt her heart quicken when she saw Luke's name on the screen.

I'm sorry. I can't make it tonight.

Sam frowned. Something was wrong. She just knew it. Luke hadn't cancelled on her for a while now. Even if he was late, he still came. And even when he had cancelled on her, he'd never done it this late. Unease spread through her. Was he preparing to leave her?

She remembered his easiness and smiles when she'd left the office that afternoon and knew that that couldn't be it. He seemed as happy as he'd ever been.

But then why had he cancelled on her? Was there another woman? She immediately chastised herself for the thought. Luke was *not* Jason—cheating was not in his character. The two might be similar on the surface, but they were completely different on the inside. She saw that now.

Jason had always had this listlessness about him that had not only propelled him to succeed, but had also made him seek out the approval of others while Luke had never particularly cared for what other people thought. All Luke had ever really cared about was Harkin.

Remembering just how focused he was when it came to work, she sighed. She was worrying for nothing. In all the time that she'd known him, Luke lived and breathed

Harkin. He probably just had something urgent he needed to take care of. Shaking her head at her own silliness, she responded to his text.

That's all right. See you tomorrow?

There was a brief pause before her phone dinged.

Yeah. I'll go to your place.

She frowned as she set her phone down and went to get her dinner from the oven. No matter how much she told herself she was making something out of nothing, she couldn't get rid of that nagging feeling that something was terribly wrong.

Luke's chest tightened as he hesitated outside of Sam's apartment two days later. He didn't want to break up with her. In fact, he couldn't remember ever being as happy as he was when he was with her.

But this was about so much more than him. He had the company and the employees to think about and they deserved more than a boss who had his head in the clouds.

He'd thought about just seeing Sam on the weekends, but he knew that that would never work. Not only did he doubt his ability to stay away from her during the week, he also knew that his mind would never be far away from her just as it's been these past two days. He hadn't seen her and yet she'd been all he'd been able to think about. He'd never had trouble concentrating on work before Sam, but she now consumed his thoughts.

And like his employees and investors, she deserved

much more than a fraction of his time. These past few months have proven that he couldn't give enough of himself to both Harkin and Sam, so it was best to let her go. The thought of a life without her was almost too much to bear, but he couldn't be selfish, gladly taking whatever he could get. He wouldn't be any better than Jason and Luke would not take advantage of Sam.

What made this all worse was the knowledge that he was going to hurt her. She might not be in love with him yet, but it was getting there. She loved being with him almost as much as he loved being with her and the fact that she'd been willing to have dinner with his parents told him that she'd been willing to make their relationship work. Hell. She'd even cooked breakfast for him even though she hated to cook. They'd been small steps forward to what he'd so desperately wanted.

But he had to do what he had to do. Without a doubt she'd find someone else soon enough. His gut clenched at the thought of her with another man, but he had to step away—for both his sake and hers.

He opened the door and found her sitting at the dining table with her laptop opened as business news played in the background. She looked up with a smile. His chest ached at the realization that he was never going to walk into her apartment to find her working again, that he'd never get to listen to her sing in the shower or wake up with her in his arms ever again.

She stood and walked towards him as he stood, frozen. He didn't want to do this.

She frowned when she was near. "What's wrong?"

"We have to break up," he said before he lost his nerve. It would be so easy to throw caution to the wind and enjoy what they had for however long they could, but he couldn't. The company deserved his full attention and she deserved someone who would put her first. "I'm sorry," he said as he shook his head. With his heart breaking, he pushed on. "I'm getting busy at the office and don't have time for a relationship right now. Harkin needs my full attention."

* * *

"Oh." Sam's throat tightened. "I understand," she said, though she didn't really.

What was wrong with her?

First, Jason had cheated because she wasn't enough for him and now Luke didn't think she was good enough, either. Because she knew Luke's talk about being busy was bull. He could've just said that he wanted to pull back and see her when things were less hectic at work, but he wasn't even offering that. He wanted out and was trying to make things easier on her by saying that he was busy. In the back of her head, she registered him hugging her, his clean scent enveloping her.

"Thank you," he murmured as he backed away. "It's been amazing."

"It's okay," she forced out. Though it was hurting like hell right now, she didn't want to be with someone who didn't want her. She'd only be setting them up both for failure. "It was just a fling anyway." She tried to brush off the significance of their relationship yet the words felt wrong. False. A mockery of every intense emotion he'd made her feel. "Friends?" she asked as she looked at him, though she knew she was only kidding herself. She would make sure she was out of his life so that she would never have to see him with another woman.

"Friends." He hesitated before giving her something.

A key. The key to her apartment.

Her heart broke. He had this all planned out, didn't he? She'd never stood a chance of changing his mind. And in that moment, she was glad she hadn't begged, glad she'd responded with dignity and composure.

"Thank you," she said numbly.

"Yeah. I'll…uh, see you around."

As soon as Luke was gone, Sam gave into the tears she'd been holding back. She didn't know how, but this hurt a lot more than when she'd found out that Jason had been cheating on her. Luke had gotten under her skin and made her love him like she'd never loved another and she feared that she'd never be right again.

Holy. That's a great buy. You have to buy it before someone else figures this out. And let me know when you're done, so I can buy some for myself!

Laying in bed, Luke smiled softly as he read the old text conversation he'd had with Sam two weeks later. He could almost hear her voice and, like the masochist he was, he couldn't stop reading them. *All of them.*

He'd cherish the memories of these past months with her for the rest of his life and hated that any new memories he'd have with her would only be as friends and he wasn't even sure if that would happen. Though they'd agreed to it, neither of them had contacted the other since they'd broken up, and he didn't expect that to change anytime soon. He'd hurt her, and she would understandably stay away from him for the time being. Or maybe not. She wouldn't have asked to be friends if she wasn't planning on following through.

At the time, he'd thought it would be hell trying to be friends, but after two weeks of not seeing her or hearing her voice, he would've killed to get a call from her. He read another text—this time of her asking what he wanted for dinner—and he knew that it was time to let her go. He'd done the right thing by breaking up with her and he just had to suck it up.

His heart breaking, he deleted the thread of messages.

A brief sense of panic overtook him as the messages disappeared right before his eyes before he hardened himself. He had to move on—not wallow. There was no point in looking back and thinking about how things could've been different. He'd just find himself missing her even more.

Knowing that he wouldn't be able to sleep anytime soon, he got out of bed. He would get rid of anything that reminded him of her. He'd never move on if he didn't.

He went to get an empty clothes basket and put everything that was hers into it—her jacket, her shirts that she'd left over… Hell. Even the presents that she and Jason had given him over the years.

He was just putting a book she'd given him for Christmas two years ago inside the basket when he remembered the ring on the top shelf of his walk-in cabinet. Not wanting to look at it, he'd put it there after it had been delivered.

He sighed as he went to get the ring. He'd been so hopeful the day he'd ordered it. He'd thought that his love could sustain them both. Stupid, stupid, stupid. Knowing that he would end up donating the ring, he briefly considered just giving it to her before he crossed out the idea and dumped it into the basket. Giving the ring to her would only lead to questions he didn't want to answer. Because at the end of the day, nothing had changed. He still couldn't have her.

He straightened and felt his chest tighten when he saw the bed—the bed he and Sam had spent countless hours cuddling in—and realized that memories of Sam filled the whole apartment and always would.

If he truly wanted to get rid of all the memories, he'd have to get a new apartment.

Samantha Johnson.

Sam frowned as she looked at the temporary paper ID. She'd thought she'd be happy when she'd finally changed her name back to her maiden one—even relieved—but all she felt was empty inside. To be honest, she'd felt empty ever since Luke had broken up with her. Being with Luke had become second nature to her, and without him, she felt lost.

Her phone rang, and she stuffed the paper in her bag then got her phone out. Nina's name flashed on the screen.

"Hey, Nina," she said as she answered the phone and stepped out of the courthouse and into the summer heat.

"Honey, what's wrong?"

She winced. She'd been so caught up in her thoughts that she'd forgotten to sound cheerful. Again. "I changed my name back to Johnson, but it doesn't seem to be sinking in yet. Perhaps it'll feel different when I get the driver's license."

"Honey, what you need is revenge sex—not a driver's license."

Guilt dug at her at the reminder of how she'd used Luke. It hadn't been fair of her to use him in such a way, but she was paying for it now.

"I did, but it didn't work out." Over time, she'd fooled herself into thinking that their relationship was something more than it really was, but in reality, it had just been a fling.

"You…wait—what? With who? When? How?"

Sam hesitated. Since the relationship hadn't worked out, she was thankful that only a handful of people knew about it. In some ways, it had made the break-up easier because she hadn't been forced to deal with people's questions and looks. But Nina was family and before all this, she'd always told Nina everything, and so, Sam murmured, "With Luke."

There was a pause before her friend answered, "You never do anything in moderation, do you? I was thinking more along the lines of a staid teacher or a doctor, but you just jumped right into the deep end."

"I don't think I'd ever be able to sleep with someone I didn't know," Sam confessed.

"I know. Casual sex isn't for everyone. Why didn't it work out? Was it bad?"

"It was amazing," Sam admitted. The best she'd ever had.

"Oh, my goodness. You fell for him, didn't you?"

"Yeah." The word barely made it out around the huge knot in her throat. After all this time, she'd thought she was done crying, but she wasn't.

"Oh, honey. I'm so sorry."

"It was my fault. I knew going in that it was just sex, but it was so easy to fall in love with him." Sam sighed. "I know I'm just being ungrateful. I finally got the clean break I wanted all those months ago. I sold the house and Jason's half of the company. I got an apartment in the city and changed my name…"

And with what happened with Luke, she doubted that he'd ever contact her again. It was truly going to be a fresh start, but this time she didn't want it. No matter how smart a clean break would be, she hated the thought of never seeing Luke again.

"But it turns out it's not what you wanted," her friend said shrewdly, as if reading her mind.

"Yeah."

"Hey, why don't you come over this weekend? You

could meet Andrew and you can help me find my wedding dress. We can look at all the bridesmaid stuff as well. You *are* going to be my maid of honor, aren't you?"

"I'd love to," Sam admitted. "But don't you think I'm the wrong choice considering everything that's happened?"

"I think you're a resilient romantic and there's no one else I'd rather have as my maid of honor."

Wedding and bridesmaids' dresses were the last things Sam wanted to be around. But for the sake of Nina, she'd put her sadness aside. "Then I'd love to."

CHAPTER TWENTY-THREE

There was a soft knock on Luke's office door before it opened. "It's almost two and you haven't eaten yet," Sheila said. "Is there something you want me to order?"

"I'm not really hungry," Luke said without looking up from the report he was reading. He wasn't in the mood to talk with anyone right now.

"All right," his assistant said before she stopped suddenly. "No. It's not all right. I tried to keep my nose out, but this is enough. What happened?"

Surprised at her outburst, Luke looked up to see the normally staid Sheila, staring daggers into him.

"Nothing happened," he said finally. "I just don't feel like eating right now." He didn't have much of an appetite.

"Whatever you said to Sam, just apologize."

His heart skipped a beat at the mention of Sam's name before he realized what his assistant had said. "You know about Sam?"

Sheila rolled her eyes as she crossed her arms. "It

doesn't take a genius to notice how cranky you were when Sam left and how happy you've been since the gala." When he didn't respond, she continued, "Just apologize for whatever you said or did, because you're really starting to scare some of the guys with all your grunting and staring."

Her words reminded him of the conversation he'd had with Sam when she came by for lunch. Little had he known that that would be the last time they'd go out with each other. He frowned when he realized something.

"You aren't bothered by me and Sam?" he asked, surprised. Jason had always been popular with the employees. Luke couldn't imagine them being accepting of him being with their beloved boss's widow.

Sheila shrugged. "It's Wall Street. You're all a little crazy. Besides, at least you didn't steal your son's girlfriend like that Rick guy," she said, referring to another hedge fund manager who'd divorced his wife so that he could marry his son's girlfriend. "I still can't believe that sick bastard." She shook her head. "Let me know if you change your mind about lunch."

Luke ran a hand through his hair once his assistant was out of the room. He knew that Sam wouldn't approve of the way he'd been acting lately, but he just felt so dead inside. It was as if he were just going through the motions.

Even the fact that Harkin was finally back on track didn't help. It was as if there was a big hole in his heart and he feared that it would never be right again. He'd heard the saying that it was better to have loved and lost than to not have loved at all, but he doubted that that person had even felt an ounce of what he did for Sam.

Because he had absolutely no clue about how he was supposed to go on without her. Sam had him so twisted inside that he couldn't sleep. All he could think about was her and not to have her… He groaned. Though he'd loved those precious months he'd had with her, he knew that it would've been better living in denial than to know what he was missing.

With that grim thought, he pushed his chaotic thoughts aside and focused on the one thing he could manage: work.

* * *

Luke had just finished taking a shower the next day when his phone beeped.

Sam.

Excitement coursed through him at the possibilities for why she'd texted him and he had to swipe the screen three times before he got it right.

Can I come up?

She was in the apartment building! Was she coming to say that he'd made a mistake and that they belonged together? Or was it just to visit and say hi? Either way, he was happy to see her.

Sure. The code is still the same and your fingerprint still works.

He hit send and quickly put on some clothes. The elevators opened just as he walked into the living room. His heart leapt and, like a man starved, he drank in the sight of her—her dark hair and those beautiful eyes. Hell. He could look at her eyes all day. He was so happy to see her that he didn't notice the box in her hands until she practically shoved it at him.

"Here are the things you left at my place."

His stomach dropped as he took hold of the box. She was getting rid of her memories of him. Had their time together meant so little to her? His throat tightened at the realization that what they had really had just been a fling to her. And though he'd suspected it, the confirmation was a blow to his chest.

"Wait. I'll get you your stuff, too," he said, instinctively pushing back. If she didn't want anything to do with him, he didn't want to have anything to do with her, either.

He got the basket he'd dumped everything into the other night and quickly went back to her. She hadn't moved from her spot a few feet in front of the elevator. He guessed she didn't want to have to stay here longer than she had to. Incensed, he almost thrust the basket at her.

Regret seized him the moment she grabbed it. He'd deleted all those messages and had nothing left of her. He was on the verge of pulling back the basket, saying that it was a mistake, when she murmured, "Thank you."

She gave him a soft smile. "Great minds, huh?"

It was too late.

"I'll see you around." She turned and walked to the elevator. He willed her to come back to him. But the elevators came and once again, she was gone.

How could this hurt so much?

Sam's chest tightened as she dropped the basket Luke had given her on the couch. They'd only been together for three months. Three months. How was it possible that him breaking up with her could affect her so? Especially after everything that had happened with Jason. Shouldn't the destruction of her marriage be the worst thing to have happened to her? Yet it wasn't.

She sighed as she ran a hand through her hair. She should've known going in not to expect that much from Luke. She knew his track record. But it was as if with every smile and every kiss Luke had given her, she'd lost a little more of herself.

Where was her pride? Her dignity? If he didn't want her, she shouldn't want him, right?

But she did. With every fiber of her being, she did. It almost seemed unfair to love someone the way she loved Luke and not have him love her back. And the way he'd so casually given her the basket of her things! He'd been so prepared. He'd probably done that to every woman he'd dated!

Unlike her, where she'd just wanted to get rid of all the memories that had made her miss him more than she could bear. She beat back tears as she looked inside the basket and picked up the red sweater she'd left at his place.

Anger suddenly burst inside of her. Maybe it was good to know how little she'd meant to him. That way, she'd get over him that much quicker. Determined to put him behind her, she took the basket and emptied its contents on her couch.

She frowned when a black box landed on top of her

sweater. She didn't remember ever giving him something so small. It looked like a jewelry box. Tension coiled in her belly as she picked it up. Was this the box those cuff links she and Jason had bought him come in? Not being able to remember anything about the cuff links except their design, she opened the box and felt as if the rug had been pulled out from under her.

A diamond ring?

Her mind raced at the reasons why Luke would have a diamond ring. Had he met someone or was he holding it for a friend? Knowing that neither Adam nor Brian had a steady girlfriend, she realized that Luke must've met someone. *That* was why he'd broken up with her. It wasn't because he was busy. It was because he'd met another woman!

Her chest ached at the thought of him marrying another woman before she realized that he never acted rashly. Luke would've never gotten a ring for someone he'd just started seeing. He was meticulous to a fault.

Rage filled her at the knowledge that he must've been seeing them both at the same time. No wonder he'd been so willing to keep their relationship a secret!

Her blood boiling, she snapped the box shut and headed towards her door. She might not have gotten to tell off Jason the way he deserved, but she'd sure relish in telling Luke!

* * *

The punching bag squeaked as it swung backwards. Luke's muscles tensed in anticipation as it came swinging back. Right hook, left punch. It squeaked as it moved away and he punched it harder when it came back, putting all his frustration into it. He *knew* he should have never started anything with Sam. He'd just been fooling himself thinking that there could be something real between them.

He gave the bag two uppercuts. How he wished that he could turn back time and stop this all from happening. His fists began to hurt, but he kept right on punching. Hurt was better than the numbness he'd been feeling ever since they'd broken up. He was so intent on hitting the bag that he almost didn't hear the elevator.

Knowing that it was probably his mom checking up on him after he'd ignored her calls earlier, he groaned. He knew he should've answered them, but he just hadn't felt like pretending as if everything was okay when it wasn't. He still hadn't told her that he and Sam weren't together. Not only did he not want his mom's pity, but admitting that they'd broken up to the only people who knew about them made it seem more final somehow. Sighing, he took off his gloves and headed towards the living room. But instead of his mom, he saw Sam storming towards him. Her eyes blazing as she thrust something at him.

"Do you care to explain what this is?" she asked.

He looked down, and felt his chest tighten at the sight of the ring.

"It's nothing," he answered. She didn't need to know that he'd been foolish enough to think that they could spend the rest of their lives together.

"It's nothing?" she parroted. "How could you do this?

To me and to this other woman? I thought you were better than this."

"What?" he asked, confused. *What other woman?*

"I can't believe you cheated on whoever you were dating with me." He hated seeing the disappointment in her eyes, especially when he wasn't the cheater. He would never take her love for granted that way. He would've gladly accepted it and spent the rest of his life making sure that she never regretted the decision.

"I've never cheated on anyone in my life," he told her, hating that she could have such a low opinion of him. "I was always true to you."

Her eyes flashed. "I can't believe this. You won't even admit it. Here, take your ring."

"Keep it," he quickly offered. He might be regretting deleting all those text messages and giving her back all her things, but he might break if he got that ring. It would only remind him of everything that he'd lost. "There's no proposal anyway."

"Well. It was nice helping you get your shit together," she said snidely. She pushed the box into his chest and walked away from him for the second time that day. His gut clenched at the thought of the woman he loved thinking so lowly of him.

"Wait," he said as he followed her. When she didn't stop, he grabbed hold of her arm, but as soon as he did, instinct took over and he kissed her.

Whether it was because of instinct, he didn't know, but she kissed him back even as he could feel the waves of anger coursing through her. But even her anger couldn't ruin the kiss because she was back in his arms.

Then, something shifted. She was softer, and he suddenly didn't feel quite so desperate. It was like they were both taking the time to learn each other's taste again. He groaned as he sunk his hands into her. Damn, how he'd missed her. Feeling as if he were home once again, he deepened the kiss, loving the taste of her, the feel of her, her…

Too soon, she was pushing him away.

"I love you," he said, hating the thought of that being the last time he ever got to taste her lips or hold her in his arms.

She laughed. "What? One proposal falls through, so you go to the next person?"

"There was never another woman," he said, frustrated. "Only you. I bought that ring for you."

She hesitated for a millisecond before hardening. "Was this before or after you broke up with me?"

"Before."

"So, after buying me a ring, you decide to break up with me? You need to work on your story more."

Fear like he'd never known spread through him when he saw that she was about to bolt.

"Don't leave," he said as he grabbed her again. "I love you," he said as he buried his face in her neck, the familiar smell of vanilla welcoming him. "I always have."

"I always have—what does *that* mean?" Sam asked, her voice suddenly wary as she pulled away to look at him.

"I've always loved you," Luke said plainly. "I don't

know what happened. I went from thinking that I should find a woman like you to wanting you. It was probably why I told you about Jason's affair all those years ago." He sighed as he ran a hand through his hair. "Okay. It *was* exactly the reason why I told you about Jason. It wasn't exactly my shining moment, but I hated that he took you for granted. It killed me each time I saw him leave the office and know that he really wasn't going to a meeting. You deserved so much more." His throat tightened. He ached to reach for her, but he knew that he didn't have that right. "It's not like I deserve you, either, but I *need* you in my life. Please don't go."

* * *

"I know I've made a mess of this, but I'm going mad inside." Luke dropped to one knee, with her hand still in his. "Will you do me the honor of becoming my wife?"

Her heart flipped at the love in his eyes. She couldn't believe what she was hearing. He loved her? "Are you serious?"

"I am. I can't imagine a life without you. I don't want a life without you. These past weeks have been absolute torture."

She shook her head, confused. "But you were the one who broke up with me!"

He grimaced. "You're too much of a distraction. It's just too easy to let things at the office go, because all I want to do is to be with you. But I found out that it's worse without you. I need you in my life, Samantha. Please say yes."

Could this be true?

Sam looked in his eyes and saw the earnestness there. She blinked back tears of gratefulness as she dropped to her knees to join him. "I didn't think that I could fall in love again, especially not after what happened with Jason," she said as she cupped his face. "But somehow, I'm more in love with you than I ever was with him. I've never been as devastated as I was these past—"

He interrupted her with a kiss and she thought that was just fine. She'd never get enough of his kisses.

"I love you," he said as he broke the kiss and met her gaze.

Joy filled her heart at the words. "I love you, too."

He laughed and they both rose and kissed each other again.

"Say it again," he said as he broke the kiss.

"I love you." He smiled before he kissed her once more. Shivers coursed through her as his hands roamed her waist before he lifted her and headed towards the bedroom.

He laid her gently on the bed. "I love you, too," he said as he cupped her face and then he proceeded to show her just how much.

EPILOGUE

A year and a half later

Luke's chest tightened as Sam walked into his office pushing the stroller. After all this time, she still had that effect on him simply by walking into a room. He didn't know how he'd gotten so lucky to have her as his wife and this beautiful, healthy baby as his daughter, but he was forever grateful. They were his everything.

It still scared him to think about how close he'd been to losing Sam.

He couldn't believe that he'd almost chosen the company over her, that he'd thought he'd had to choose. Sure, it had taken some time to get used to delegating his work to others, but it hadn't been as hard as he'd thought— especially when it meant he'd get to free up his time to spend with Sam.

He stood to kiss his wife. Sam's cheeks were flushed when he pulled away and he couldn't help but smile at the realization that he still affected her, too.

"Is she sleeping?" he asked as he nodded at Suzie, their baby girl.

Sam smiled. "No. She woke up somewhere around the trading floor. Everyone just had to see her." Though the press had been critical of his and Sam's relationship—even saying that they'd been seeing each other while Jason had been alive, the employees had been surprisingly accepting.

Adam had said it was because Luke was an easier boss to work with now that he'd married Sam, but Luke thought that the employees were just happy to have Sam back at the office. Either way, he was grateful. He didn't want anyone to treat his daughter differently, because of who her parents had fallen in love with.

He bent down and saw beautiful dark eyes just like her mother's look at him from under the cover.

"Hi there, baby girl," he said as he brought his hand in front of her. His chest tightened as Suzie's eyes widened as she smiled and grabbed his hand.

"I have a meeting in ten minutes," Sam said. In addition to her managing money for her friends and family, she also managed a portion of the company's portfolio. "Did you want to watch her, or should I get Brenda? She's downstairs flirting with Ruben again."

Luke laughed at the thought about their babysitter flirting with the security guard. "Leave them be. I think we can find something to do." As if agreeing with him, Suzie clapped and kicked her feet.

"Thanks." Sam came over to give him a quick peck on the lips, but he had other ideas. He turned the stroller so that they were facing its back and wrapped an arm around Sam, deepening the kiss. She had ten minutes, after all.

Thanks so much for reading *Unspoken Desires!* I hope you enjoyed it. To hear about my new releases, sign up for my mailing list at natashagrace.com

BUSINESS BEFORE PLEASURE

Olivia Montgomery should be thrilled when she's put in charge of renovating The Mansion. She's wanted to restore her grandfather's old hotel back to its original glory for years. Unfortunately, its new owner, Adam Campbell, has other plans. Instead of restoring the hotel, he wants to gut it, and Olivia can't let that happen. She'll do whatever it takes to preserve her grandfather's vision. But when Adam realizes what she's up to, he decides to keep a close eye on her. A real close eye.